DHRUV

Karan Verma is a bestselling author, public speaker and dynamic young entrepreneur. His first novel *Jack & Master*, a national bestseller, continues to inspire readers across the country. A software engineer and business management postgraduate, Karan has mentored thousands of students, corporates and businesses across the globe. A recipient of various awards and titles, including the 'Youth Idol' award, Karan enjoys massive popularity amongst the youth and promises to continue scripting more stories and accomplishments.

DHRUV
LOVE STORY OF AN ALCHEMIST

KARAN VERMA

Published by
Rupa Publications India Pvt. Ltd 2020
7/16, Ansari Road, Daryaganj
New Delhi 110002

Sales Centres:
Allahabad Bengaluru Chennai
Hyderabad Jaipur Kathmandu
Kolkata Mumbai

Copyright © Karan Verma 2020

All rights reserved.

No part of this publication may be reproduced, transmitted,
or stored in a retrieval system, in any form or by any means,
electronic, mechanical, photocopying, recording or otherwise,
without the prior permission of the publisher.

This is a work of fiction. Names, characters, places and incidents are either the
product of the author's imagination or are used fictitiously and any resemblance to
any actual person, living or dead, events or locales is entirely coincidental.

ISBN: 978-93-5333-858-9

Second impression 2020

10 9 8 7 6 5 4 3 2

The moral right of the author has been asserted

Printed at HT Media Ltd, Gr. Noida

This book is sold subject to the condition that it shall not,
by way of trade or otherwise, be lent, resold, hired out, or otherwise
circulated, without the publisher's prior consent, in any form
of binding or cover other than that in which it is published.

*To Mom, the alchemist of my life,
my mentor, guide and everything.*

Chapter 1

The Boy Who Lived

A broken bottle cap, a blood-stained muslin cloth, a throbbing, pulsating anxiety and a charred soul—the situation was getting grimmer by the minute in the quaint city of Banaras. The weather hadn't been too kind, only to be worsened by one of the bloodiest ethnic clashes in recent times.

Along the holy ghats of Banaras, there stood a young couple, wrecked by chaos and sieged by fear. The lady, in her final month of pregnancy, was now in labour. The immense onslaught of pain had pulverized her into submission. The husband stood by, seemingly stoic and poised. However, his sheer helplessness to get the better of city strife and the torrid weather broke him from inside.

He kept reiterating, 'I'll get you there. Don't worry.' But with every single utterance, his gumption plummeted to abysmal depths.

Hiding beneath a torn cardboard cut-out, under a banyan tree, they peeped through the punctured holes to witness a sight both gruesome and gory. The street close to the ghat was spattered with blood and covered in ruins. Thatched huts had been decimated by violent mobs. Heart-thumping sloganeering and brutal scuffles had ripped apart the very fabric of the place. The lady, meanwhile, had started moaning in pain. Sweating profusely, writhing in agony, her knees just gave in to her weight, accentuated by her bloated belly. With a crashing thud, she lay semi-conscious on the road.

The husband somehow managed to pull her out of harm's way to a spot behind the trunk of the banyan tree, as the clashes continued. His eyes feverishly browsed for help as he sneaked down the slope, helping his wife along. Her eyelids were drooping and her breath kept getting heavier. Sighing in vain, the husband cried desperately for help, only to be ambushed by a frenzied mob. The deafening sirens of the police vans and the heavy downpour upped the chaos as an insensitive and mindless mob began running helter-skelter. Things got uglier when the mob crashed head first into the man who, went down with a violent thud. His upper lip busted and blood started pouring out from his mouth. The man's eyes tried to focus and locate his wife despite his blurred vision. To his horror, he saw her lying unconscious a few feet away.

'Rukmani!' he shouted with horror, as someone in the headless mob recklessly kicked her face. Nobody heard the man's cry as he tried to reach out for his wife. The holy ghats of Banaras were witness to the heart-wrenching desperation of a man seeking help, but that day, humanity had, for some strange reason, eluded the city, which many believed was the birthplace of mankind. The man was bruised and battered, his shirt had been torn apart. Striving through several knocks from the running crowd, he finally reached his wife, Rukmani. She lay comatose. Her face was bruised and scarred, a stream of red flowing from her mouth. A chill ran down her husband's spine. *She is still breathing,* he observed. Jittering with anxiety, he lifted her in his arms. Dumbstruck and helpless, the man was bleeding himself, as he struggled through the imbroglio.

Just then, he heard his wife say something. 'Ram! Ram!' she called out her husband's name. He replied, 'Nothing will happen to you, please hold on.' His throat was choked and so was the way out from the Tulsi Ghat. Meanwhile, a few natives had been observing Ram and Rukmani and they finally came out to help the beleaguered couple. The police meanwhile had managed to exercise some control. Rukmani's condition was getting serious with every passing second. With no hospital close by and the profuse bleeding refusing to stop, the local ladies huddled together. The lightning continued flashing as dark clouds hovered above the city, and more so around the fortune of this couple.

Ram Samrat was a simple man of humble means. A trader of mystic stones and gems, he lived in a small village called Akhari in Banaras, with his wife Rukmani. After years of prayers, fasts and rituals, they were blessed with the good news of Rukmani's pregnancy. Little did they know that the day that was supposed to be their most special one, would turn into one of gruesome massacres.

Ram waited on as the ladies attended to an ailing Rukmani Devi. His fellow natives cajoled and consoled him but deep down they were all aware that some serious damage had been inflicted on Rukmani. She had suffered acute head injuries and had lost a lot of blood. A miscarriage seemed inevitable as things kept getting complicated for her. Ram's tears did not stop and neither did the innumerable thoughts flashing through his mind. Crippled with fear and negativity, he slipped into a limbo, only to be rudely shaken by blood-curdling cries outside. Ram's heart pounded with a catastrophic ferocity as he rushed towards the site.

'Rukmani is sinking!' shouted a woman, breaking down in front of Ram. Huffing with anxiety, Ram asked the medical attendant about his wife's condition. He did not respond. There was a sense of panic, which was exponentially spreading its tentacles and taking everybody in its maniacal sweep. Ram's friends and relatives, who had reached the spot by then, tried to hold him together as the cries and despair of the ladies kept growing manyfold. The thunderous strikes of lightning continued as Ram resigned to his fate and awaited the unfolding of what was going to be an extremely long night in his life. It was a doomed night, the naysayers had prophesied. Many astrologers believed that the planetary positions and the moon were in a conflicted state that day. In other places, such observations could be passed off as vile imagination, but in Banaras, prophecies and cosmic signs were a part of the mystical ethos of the place.

And then came the dreaded news. Rukmani Devi could not be saved. Right there along the Tulsi Ghat, she breathed her last.

Ram was a devastated man as he painfully howled his heart out. He broke down and totally fell apart as the people around tried consoling him in vain. However, the complete news was yet to trickle in. Amidst the howls, the cries of anguish and the crashing thunder in the skies, a squeaky little cry was heard, which momentarily silenced everyone.

It was a boy. Strange were the ways of destiny as Rukmani Devi, against all man-made and natural odds, left behind a baby boy along the holy ghats of Banaras. Ram's tears kept rolling down his face; his howls however halted for a while as he saw the little boy in the arms of the medical attendant standing by. He finally held the child in his arms. It was a moment he and Rukmani had long awaited in their dreams. Alas, when it happened, Rukmani wasn't there…

The next morning saw Rukmani's final rites being performed at the Manikarnika Ghat. Rukmani Devi, a pious lady who had always dreamt of a complete family, left for the heavenly abode, or perhaps was reborn somewhere else if the Hindu beliefs were to be believed. The local priests, sages and village folk wondered how the boy had survived against all planetary and cosmic odds. He was still under intensive medical care. However, call it the prayers of his parents or the grace of destiny, the child was finally in a stable condition after five days.

Ram's tears hadn't dried up yet. The man had gone into a shell, but his little boy's sparkling eyes imparted a fresh lease of life. There was a radiant little smile on the boy's lips, which added magnificence to his already glowing face. Oblivious to the frenzy around, oblivious to the rights and wrongs of the universe, the little boy looked up at his father with an innocent inquisitiveness as if trying to figure out his father's state of mind. The father gently kissed him and silently prayed for his well-being. As Ram reached home with his little boy, they were received and consoled by the neighbours. However, the surprise of the local priests hadn't yet died down. They were curious to view the child's birth chart.

'Born on a full moon against the wrath of planet Saturn,' they murmured with astonishment. The priest had warned Ram about the repercussion of the birth, but then perhaps it was destined. After visiting the temple and performing some customary rites, Ram went to the Dashashwamedha Ghat to seek blessings for his child from one of the most renowned priests of Banaras. The priest sat perched on his cushion in an open veranda. Around half a dozen other priests and relatives waited on tenterhooks. They were all curious to hear the priest's prophecy about the boy who had survived the wrath of the planets on that ill-fated cusp of a full moon. The priest himself was curious. This Hindu ritual was called the naming ceremony, where an appropriate name was given to a newborn vis-à-vis their birth chart and planetary positions. The little child, bundled in a red linen cloth, lay in front of the seer. There was a sense of mysticism around the boy. His face had a certain radiance, which was magnetic. The ceremony commenced as Ram and his relatives waited for the priest's pronouncement. The priest carefully drew the birth chart and studied it amidst pin drop silence. The frown lines on his forehead spoke volumes about how neck-deep he was into his analysis. After minutes of carefully scrutinizing the chart, he got up from his cushion and bent over to drink some water from an earthen pot nearby. Clearing his throat, the priest picked up the child in his arms as everyone looked towards him in anticipation.

'He is no ordinary child,' spelled out the priest, loud and clear. Ram was inquisitive to know what this meant as the priest continued, 'The child will shine like a star in the sky, bright and magnificent in its glory.' The priest's conviction was palpable in his voice, trembling with emotion. 'And henceforth this shining star shall be named "Dhruv",' announced the priest with elan.

'Dhruv...' the father wondered aloud, as the priest came towards him. A prophetic smile adorned his bearded face.

In a commanding voice, he told the father, 'Ram, your child is going to shine so bright that he is going to illuminate the universe. His written and spoken words will make the Gods sit up and take notice. When he will speak, the Gods will listen.' The entire gathering was abuzz with the priest's startling words. Ram was overwhelmed as he bent down to seek the priest's blessings. The priest graciously blessed him and said. 'Let's all pray for the well-being and prosperity of this child, who shall now be officially named "Dhruv Samrat".'

'*Jai ho!* (May you be victorious!)' reverberated the chorus, and thus began the saga of Dhruv Samrat.

Chapter 2

Dreams on Fire

'We must all become good citizens of the country.' A round of half-baked applause immediately followed. However, much to the horror of the audience, the speaker wasn't done. 'We must always be honest and speak the truth.' The precious pearls of wisdom kept raining as the agony of little children from St. Mary's Junior School continued. The young students had assembled in the open field to witness a moustached, middle-aged man, giving them life lessons and sharing noble thoughts.

Continuing his speech, he said, 'Life is a journey and...' At that moment, one of the kids finally succumbed to the heat of the sun and the moral suffocation of the sermon, as he fainted amidst the assembly. Chaos ensued amongst the students; but such was the moral commitment of the speaker, that he continued telling them how to live a successful life. A couple of teachers and a friend of the boy carried him out of the gathering. As the teacher lifted him in his arms, the boy stealthily opened one of his eyes and winked at his friend. The friend couldn't control his smile and with an impish grin, he helped the teacher in carrying the boy off. As they reached the backstage, the teacher asked worriedly, 'Dhruv? Dhruv? Are you okay? Dhruv?'

Dhruv's smile was now reaching his ears. However, he

tossed and turned, so that he could hide his face. 'Yes... Yes... Sir, I am feeling better,' he faintly said, covering his face with his hands. His friend Sudama, standing next to them, was struggling to control an insane bout of laughter. Dhruv, who meanwhile, had started opening his eyes slowly and rather melodramatically, said, 'Oh Sir, I am feeling so bad, I just missed the remaining part of the chief guest's speech.'

The irony had Sudama rolling in laughter behind the backs of the teachers. Barely able to hold it, Sudama said, 'Sir, don't worry, Dhruv will be fine. I will be with him backstage. You please join the gathering.' The teachers checked up on Dhruv again and entrusting Sudama with the responsibility, they left. As soon as they were out of earshot, the boys started chuckling and high-fived each other.

'Woohoo!' cried out Dhruv. 'Now that's what you call a performance, unlike the one you gave last time when we had a special guest,' he said. 'And by the way, next time, if the guest lecturer is boring, you're going to bail us out!'

'Oh, come on! My quota for the term is over,' claimed Sudama.

'Hell no!' shouted Dhruv.

'Yes!' Sudama shouted back.

'No!'

'Yes!'

'No!'

The words flew back and forth, as the boys started quarrelling. Seemingly innocent on the surface, their intensity was ferocious as they grabbed each other by the scruff of their necks. And just when they were in the middle of their fight, the teachers came back to check on Dhruv's condition.

To their surprise, they saw before them a fighting fit

Dhruv, a far cry from the fragile child who had fainted some time back. Two minutes later, both the boys were standing outside the class, holding their ears, with their arms looped around their legs, a traditional Indian punishment.

'Friends again?' asked Dhruv, extending his hand, his head still trapped between his legs. His large expressive eyes were waiting to hear an answer.

'Yes, but you should be more careful,' warned Sudama, as they shook hands and nodded in unison.

'At least we are better off here, rather than listening to the genius special guest,' said Dhruv.

'That we are,' laughed Sudama, who always had a problem controlling his bouts of laughter. Soon the school bell rang as Dhruv and Sudama ran out singing and whistling aloud.

Dhruv was a loveable, mischievous boy, the only child brought up by a single father, Ram Samrat. He was the darling of the villagers of Akhari. Vibrant and extremely inquisitive, the boy was quite a storyteller and always had some trick or the other up his sleeve. His best friend was a poor Dalit boy named Sudama.

Sudama's mother would take care of the boys during the day, till Dhruv's father, Ram, would come back from work in the evening. Dhruv and Sudama would sit by the ghats for hours together, playing around, having fun and, at times, talking their hearts out.

'Sudama…sometimes I wonder why you were named "Sudama",' said Dhruv, plucking a dead blade of grass from the soil, as they sat by the famous Assi Ghat.

'Why, what's wrong with that?' asked Sudama, standing a

few feet away and glancing towards the holy Ganges.

'I was reading the fabled Krishna-Sudama story, yesterday. And you know, people generally do not name their children "Sudama",' pointed out Dhruv.

'Is it because he was poor and hungry?' asked Sudama, turning his head toward Dhruv.

'Hmmm... Yes, it is considered a bad omen,' informed Dhruv.

'More than a bad omen, I see it as the truth in my case,' said a dejected Sudama, as he sat down staring at the waves rather despondently. 'Dhruv, my mother tells me that it will be difficult to pay my school fees this time.'

'So, will you leave me and go to some other school?' asked Dhruv.

'I don't know. Mother says that we don't have money. How much money do you have, Dhruv?' asked Sudama, inquisitively and rather naively.

'Hmm... I will ask father about it today, but please don't leave me Sudama. Who would I laugh around with and who would... (Dhruv began gasping for breath) who would—I don't know—play with me?' Dhruv fumbled for words, almost on the brink of breaking down.

Sudama's voice also cracked a little and before he could speak further, he started sobbing silently. 'Dhruv, you are the only upper-caste boy who talks to me.' Big, diamond-like tears, started rolling down his cheeks.

'Upper-caste? Who told you that nonsense?' asked Dhruv, confused and infuriated at the same time.

'Ask some of the priests and sadhus. Many of them don't even make eye contact with us,' pointed out Sudama.

Dhruv stood in silence, mulling over what Sudama had

said. Perhaps his young mind was discovering some unfortunate realities that defied logic but were deeply entrenched in our society.

'Sudama, I sometimes wonder who made all this high caste, low caste demarcation. Was it God who did this?' he inquired.

'Maybe... I think he created everything,' said Sudama matter-of-factly.

'Hmm... So, for whatever wrong is happening, God is to be blamed!' exclaimed Dhruv, with a strange kind of renewed energy.

'Oh yes,' Sudama shared his passion. 'I am not doing my homework; who is to be blamed?'

'God!' shouted out Dhruv.

'You not cleaning your study room; who is to be blamed?'

'God!' they shouted in unison.

'Me not brushing my teeth?'

'God!'

'Oh it feels so much better! Woohoo!' exclaimed Sudama.

'That's it! Whatever wrong is happening or not working out, let's blame it on God and have fun,' Dhruv chuckled innocently. Their innocent yet thoughtful jibes dissolved into the blood-red sunrays, as evening set in along the ghats of Banaras.

Ram Samrat, ever since his wife's death, had become a reticent shadow of his former self. The seer's words about Dhruv would echo in his mind every now and then.

'Baba! Baba!' called out Dhruv as he entered, lifting the latch of the knee-high door and running through the kitchen garden, right into his father's arms. Ram gently kissed him and seated him on his lap.

'Baba, how much money do we have?' he asked. Ram had a hearty laugh at the question as Dhruv waited for the figure on tenterhooks.

'Is there something you need?' enquired Ram.

'No Baba, just generally I want to know,' Dhruv said.

'Well, we have enough, perhaps,' said Ram, a man of limited means.

Pat came another question: 'What is "enough," Baba?'

'Oh God, your questions never run out, do they?'

Dhruv's twinkling eyes sparkled even more whenever he asked a question. Ram smiled and said, 'You know, son, your mother always used to say that there can be enough money in the world for one's needs but never enough for one's desires.'

'That's deep, Baba. You talk like the chief guest who came to our school.'

'Haha!' laughed out Ram, cuddling Dhruv warmly. Ram did not stop smiling, though deep down something had stirred in him. Probably they were Rukmani's memories.

'Baba, are you thinking about Ma?' asked Dhruv, gently rubbing his head. Ram ruffled his hair and said, 'Yes, I am, and that's the last question of the day.'

'One more thing, one more thing, Baba!' Dhruv said frantically, as he slid down from his father's lap. 'Baba, all through the village, there is a strange kind of mystique around what our forefathers used to do,' said Dhruv. His innocent mind found it difficult to fathom such things. 'What did our forefathers do, Baba?'

The question set a thousand thoughts flashing across Ram's mind. 'Where do you keep hearing this nonsense?' Ram dismissed the query. 'Don't you know we deal in metals and stones?'

'I know that, Baba,' Dhruv said, almost in tears at not being able to comprehend clearly. 'But they tell me that our forefathers were special people.' His eyes popped at the word 'special'.

A minute of silence followed, after which Ram seated Dhruv on his lap again. Dhruv's eyes however were resolute enough to not lose focus from the question and get distracted by anything else.

'Alright... Alright...' said his father, exhaling deeply.

'Dhruv...' He paused for a second. 'Now listen to me carefully... Legend goes that your forefathers were gifted enough to convert lead into gold,' he said, weighing every word.

'Gold... Wow!' exclaimed Dhruv, with astonishment. 'That's magic, Baba! Were our forefathers magicians?' he asked.

'Call it magic or call it divine perseverance,' said the father, reflecting deeply. 'Or...' Ram paused. 'There is one more name to them—they're called alchemists.'

'Al-che-mist,' Dhruv was trying hard to repeat the word.

'But, Dhruv, remember not to talk about this with the village people,' cautioned Ram. Dhruv gently placed a finger on his lips.

'Alright now, Dhruv, time to go to sleep.'

'Baba...' whispered Dhruv. With a parched throat yet a steely resolve, he said, 'I want to grow up and become an alchemist.'

Ram smiled and gently kissed him on his forehead. 'Son, that art has long been lost with your forefathers. You know what you are going to grow up and become?' he asked.

Dhruv shook his head. 'Come, I will show you', said Ram, taking him to the kitchen garden of their house. It was one of those starry evenings of Banaras, when the mystique of the ghats blended and sparkled along with the glittering sky.

'You see those up there, Dhruv?' Ram pointed out.

'Yes Baba, they are called stars,' said Dhruv, happy that he actually knew at least something that evening.

'You know Dhruv, out of all those stars, there is one star that shines the brightest of them all… It's called the Dhruv-Star.'

'Woah,' the boy chuckled hearing his name and felt elated at the discovery. He hugged his father and sitting there on the platform, he told him, 'Baba, I promise you, one day I am going to become so big and shine so bright that even Ma up there will be able to see me.'

The father blessed his child with all the luck and success, as the glittering night in Banaras witnessed the first sparks of genius, both sacred and pure.

'Al-che-mist,' spelled out Dhruv, as Sudama carefully listened.

'What does this word even mean?' Sudama asked.

'I will tell you sometime—' began Dhruv, but before he could complete what he was saying, the class teacher walked in carrying a pile of report cards. Those rectangular green-coloured cards were enough to silence even the noisiest of classes.

'Oh my God, Dhruv!' exclaimed Sudama, almost about to cry with nervousness. 'I don't want to fail,' his lips were trembling, as he uttered those words. Dhruv closed his eyes and with folded palms, he began praying, both for himself and Sudama.

'Alright class...' the teacher announced, as if ringing a warning bell for the times to come. She continued, 'Class V-C has done well overall and all of you have passed, except for one.' The students remained frozen in anticipation, as the teacher put on her spectacles and browsed through the pile placed on the table in front. 'So, let me first start with the top three position holders.'

Amidst cheers and claps, the third- and second-rankers of the class were awarded their report cards.

And then the teacher took a deep breath and announced, 'The topper of class V-C and, in fact, the topper of all four sections is Dhruv Samrat.'

Little Dhruv's joy knew no bounds. His cheerful smile adorned by a few missing milk teeth, was now reaching his ears, as he walked up to receive his report card. Though generally a victim of Dhruv's mischief, the teacher that day just smiled and blessed the boy with success and, of course, more power to his never-ending questions.

One by one, all the report cards were distributed except for one. Roll number 39 was missing. It was Sudama's. His worst nightmare had just come true. Stony-faced and resigned, Sudama kept sitting in shock. Dhruv's joy and jubilation vaporized in no time. Sudama's face was changing colour with every passing second until he dropped his head and started crying profusely. He just didn't stop. His fellow classmates rallied around him but to no avail. Dhruv was too dumbstruck to even offer him any sympathies.

Crying in pain, Sudama mumbled, 'I will now have to discontinue my studies.' He kept sobbing and howling uncontrollably. The teacher hugged him and tried her best to calm his nerves. Soon the school bell rang and the children went running out to share their grades and progress with their parents. Some were happy, others a bit apologetic and then there were some like Sudama who wished the bell had never rung. Sudama began his long gloomy walk from the classroom to the school gate. Cheerful parents and their smiling faces continued stinging him. Tears kept rolling down from his eyes. His parents were anyway finding it difficult to pay for his education and his failure was pretty much the final nail in the coffin. As Sudama passed through the school ground, he could faintly see his father outside the gate, which was still a mile away. His heart missed a beat... Perhaps it sank every time it didn't beat. And then, from behind, he heard a voice calling his name.

'Sudama... Sudama...' Dhruv came running from behind. Dhruv hadn't seen him all this while.

Sudama broke down again when he saw Dhruv. 'Dhruv, it's all over... It's all over,' he cried and hugged Dhruv.

'Where were you?' asked Sudama. 'Oh I am sorry—congratulations. Don't want to keep you waiting, Dhruv,' said Sudama. Dhruv winced in helplessness and wished he could correct everything.

'I couldn't face you, Sudama, and I felt so miserable. Oh God, I wish, I could lend you some of my marks,' cried Dhruv.

'It's all over, Dhruv,' Sudama repeated for the third time. 'I can't face my father,' he sighed.

Dhruv himself was in tears seeing his friend's plight. But, before he could utter any more words of consolation, a group of his classmates joyously huddled around him to celebrate his success. Dhruv couldn't take his eyes off his friend, as he was dragged away by an enthusiastic lot of classmates, who were too naive to think about Sudama at that point.

A tearful goodbye, a heartbroken child trying to come to terms with a dreaded six-letter word, 'failed', and a not-so-jubilant class topper—the visual played on young Dhruv's impressionable mind for a long time. Dhruv wasn't like other children of his age. Yes, he was naughtier, but then he also had an emotional depth that was rare.

Mouth-watering candies and treats awaited him at home, but contrary to the celebratory mood, he was disillusioned seeing Sudama's failure.

'Baba...' called out Dhruv, sitting on Ram's lap and playing with a superhero action figure. 'Did you ever fail?' he naively asked.

The question had so many layers and it got Ram reflecting on his life. Ram smiled and said, 'Yes son, we all do.'

Astonished, Dhruv asked, 'Really, Baba? Which class?' He kept aside his action figure.

Ram laughed out and gently kissed him on his forehead. 'It wasn't a class, son. It was the theatre of life,' he said in a low voice. His voice continued descending in pitch, and a barrage of thoughts assailed his mind. Visuals of that fateful day when he couldn't save his wife, Rukmani, began tormenting him.

Dhruv broke the silence and asked, 'Baba, why can't I donate some of my marks to Sudama, so that he can pass? I really hated seeing him leave.'

Ram had little to say to the child. He just gently caressed his hair and said, 'You'll get your answers, son.'

Chapter 3

The Green-eyed Girl

Years passed away and Dhruv's inquisitiveness and penchant for seeking answers didn't waver an iota. If anything, it became more profound and manifested itself in various creative expressions. Dhruv Samrat had grown up to be a high-school topper of the state. Not only that, he had evolved into a famous theatre playwright in Banaras.

Banaras being a metaphor for civilization and culture, had, for centuries, exuded a rare ethos, which caught the fancy of many a thinker, artist and philosopher. Dhruv too wasn't left untouched by the mystique of the spiritual capital of India.

Along the Manikarnika Ghat, the Annual Cultural Fest became a microcosm for the glorious vibrancy of Banaras. The gathering was abuzz with enthusiasm and enriching ideas as the fest unfolded feverishly. Amidst applause and throbbing anticipation, young Dhruv came out with his troupe. Confident about his written and spoken word, the young man greeted the audience and grabbed a microphone to address the house. Dhruv was the narrator of the play, which he had conceived and scripted. The play was a scorching portrayal of a student's life and was a touching tale of how a student's dreams and aspirations are sacrificed at the altar of the pragmatism and vagaries of life, and raised the bigger question of how many students actually ended up doing what they wanted to do.

The riveting play, embellished with Dhruv's stirring narration, won over the audience and made them reflect on a range of issues. As the curtains drew to a close, Dhruv came back on the stage to a round of rapturous applause. His troupe bowed before the audience, as he took to the podium and summed up the spirit of the aspirational students of Banaras.

'My name is Dhruv...' He smiled rather impishly and continued, '"Dhruv" means a shining star. In fact, not just a shining star but the brightest star in the galaxy up there. In my humble way, ladies and gentlemen, I want to shine so bright that my Ma up there can see me.'

Tear-filled eyes and a passion-ridden voice continued to march along the corridors of people's imagination as Dhruv continued, 'I want to be a storyteller. Connecting with audiences like you and telling you a story is divine fulfilment for me. The medium doesn't matter to me. Today it's theatre, tomorrow it could be celluloid or anything else, but what matters is this spark to create and connect with people and that, for me, is my aspiration.'

'What's yours?' he asked with elan, eliciting thunderous response, as the boy wonder went on. 'The question really is—should our life be defined by a six-letter word, C A R E E R, or should it be defined by the ten-letter word C-O-N-V-I-C-T-I-O-N? For me, it's the latter and for thousands sitting here, they wish it was the latter, but alas, they are scared to face the music. So am I, but I still try my best with whatever I have.'

Dhruv's words were so mesmerizing that at times they seemed like a perfectly executed orchestra piece. Not a word here, not a note there, just the right pitch, right modulation and bang from the heart. He continued, 'Also, friends, please keep an eye out for our next blockbuster play, titled "Jack & Master". It is an adaptation of a bestseller. Hope to see you there!' Dhruv signed off with a sparkling smile.

Ram was a proud father, as he joined the gathering in a round of applause for the young students embarking on the journey of their lives. However, with every outburst of elation, Ram also grew insecure about his own health, which had begun failing him. He feared that his ailing health and escalating medical expenses could prove to be the biggest roadblock in Dhruv's path to glory. Dhruv, on the other hand, was driven to achieve what he believed was his destiny. He was the brightest child in Banaras, many believed. A rare combination of academic brilliance and artistic genius.

However, those who knew him closely vouched for the fact that Dhruv's greatest asset was not his academic brilliance, it wasn't his oratorical prowess and neither was it his passionate pursuit of his conviction; it was his heart made up of pure gold and beating with compassion for the unprivileged. Barely had the dust settled and the applause waned into cherished memories, that Dhruv received a letter in a beige envelope with the initials 'N.Y.F.A.' The boy from Banaras had just received a call letter for the coveted New York Film Academy. His application had been accepted and to top it all, he was granted a fully paid scholarship.

Dhruv couldn't believe his eyes, which dropped a tear of gratitude—a tear for dreams fuelled by passion and desire. Between his eyes welling up and the falling of the tear, a million thoughts flashed across the corridor of his mind. His thoughts and expressions were about to get a cathartic platform; the wheels of his career were all set to roll in the direction of his dreams. And just as the falling tear moistened the crisp letter in his hand, reality woke up and kissed the dreams goodbye. The sight of his ailing father, Ram, who had no one in the world except for Dhruv and unpaid debts rattled him to a pensive disposition.

Who would take care of Baba? This question was doing the rounds of his impressionable mind of eighteen. Dhruv started breathing heavily and before he could begin to weigh his options again, a little voice inside admonished him to the point of guilt.

'How can you, even for a second, think of going to la-la land, leaving Baba behind?' was the disdainfully uttered question in his mind. As realization cemented its roots, it dawned on Dhruv that his Baba's health wouldn't allow him to even go across to the other side of the Ganges.

The next few days saw Dhruv at a strange crossroads in life. The boy was flooded with offers from media and arts institutes across the country and the globe. Ram's chronic cough and escalating debts hadn't worried him as much as his son's stunned silence over the last few days. Dhruv's prophetic play on a student's career dilemma had perhaps found its real-life protagonist.

Dhruv didn't want to unnecessarily guilt-trip his Baba by throwing light on how he had prioritized his responsibilities towards his father and not his own dreams. However, Ram's faltering vision had gained enough worldly insight to see through it. Alas, he was helpless.

Ram had borrowed heavily to set up a unit for manufacturing mystic stones and pearls. Some thought it was a reckless misadventure, others cast aspersions on his business acumen, but the truth was, it was a desperate misfired attempt by a father to do all he could for his son's dreams. However, things didn't fall in line with his expectations. His health, too, deserted him at a testing time.

Irony died a thousand deaths when one of Banaras's brightest students began running out of options. However, he wasn't one of those who would throw in the towel and give up. The boy believed it was his destiny to rise above every obstacle that came his way. He took up a course in literature and liberal arts at the local Banaras Hindu University to keep his passion alive. Dhruv had always been a survivor, right from the day he was born. Months ripened into years as Dhruv valiantly tried to protect his father and his dreams, the only two possessions he had in the world. Ram had become frighteningly frail, a stark contrast to the ever-swelling debts that had engulfed him.

On the verge of completing his graduation, with insecurities looming large, the only resort to solace that Dhruv had was the stage and his gift for storytelling. Dhruv had continued to churn out gem after gem and if anything, his craft became more profound with time. A bright talent continued its bottled existence mired in the confines of grim circumstances.

The law of the cosmos is such that when life begins to come to a standstill and desires continue dying a thousand deaths, an event is triggered by the forces of the universe. 'The Canvas of Life' was the title of Dhruv's next play. Grandly titled, the play chronicled the delicious ironies of life. It also highlighted the sacredness of family bonds and relationships; perhaps stemming from the vacuum in Dhruv's life. After a couple of hours, the curtains came down and Dhruv closed yet another successful play.

As much as Dhruv relished his moment of solitude after

every cathartic play, he didn't mind answering questions and reciprocating the love he received backstage.

Amidst a swarm of inquisitive well-wishers and theatre lovers, there was a young lady waiting to speak to him. Dhruv saw her from the corner of his eye. So elegantly poised was she, that Dhruv already finalized 'The Charming Princess' as the title of his next play. Her hazel-green eyes had an enchanting sparkle, second only to the luminance of her silken-smooth hair neatly tied up in a vertical bun. She was wearing an A-line, ankle-length, floral printed skirt, with a white knotted top.

Dhruv meanwhile continued exchanging niceties with the people, wishing they could all just vanish in thin air, as he continued trying hard to catch glimpses of the young lady.

Different aspects of her struck him one by one. A couple of softly curled strands had escaped her bun and were flirtatiously caressing her angular face adorned with a sparkling smile. They swayed as she moved her head. It was divinity in motion. She had a tattoo of Goddess Venus on her right shoulder, under which was etched the word 'Emma'. Dhruv couldn't wait to speak to her.

What does she want to tell me? Did she also like the play as much as others? Dhruv's anticipation was going through the roof, as one by one, he greeted everybody backstage, and then…the girl was gone.

Dhruv frantically looked around, as more people came pouring in to see him. He clenched his teeth and winced in desperation. He wanted to see her no matter what. And then, as if a divine epiphany struck him, he put aside all protocol and bolted past everyone through the gallery, much to their surprise. He was in a different celestial orbit. He just wanted to meet the green-eyed girl. He sped past the lobby…she wasn't there. The green room...she wasn't there either.

The lady meanwhile too had an epiphany of sorts when she was walking past the gallery. She too felt a strange urge, which began to grow with every passing second. A magnetic pull drew her towards Dhruv, as she walked back past the green room. She went looking for him, but he was in the polar opposite direction, frantically looking for her.

To the bystander, it seemed like a scene straight out from a comedy of errors. However, to a philosopher, their rendezvous was the waltz of romance where if the commencement had so much mystique, one wondered what the end would be like.

And then they finally met... Both were short of breath, anxious and relieved at the same time.

'Phew!' Dhruv breathed out with relief. *She is gorgeous*, he thought.

The lady gently smiled at him. The two were yet to speak, but the sparkle of their chemistry was busy scripting something up there in the cosmos. What was it that was pulling her towards him—was it his magnetic theatrical prowess, was it his conduct or was it just an inner calling beyond any logical constructs of comprehension?

Dhruv finally broke the ice and said, 'Have we met before or something?'

The girl smiled and said, 'Not that I can remember.' Her contagious smile was slowly inching towards uninhibited laughter.

'Me neither. Hi, I am Dhruv,' he said, extending his right hand, and still catching his breath.

'I'm Emma... Emma Schellenberg,' she replied. 'I am guessing we've met in some other life, maybe,' she said rather matter-of-factly.

Dhruv couldn't quite believe what he had just heard. 'Yeah right, some other life or maybe in some parallel universe or maybe the aura of Banaras has begun playing on your mind,' he laughed. Emma too laughed out, adding chorus to an atmosphere marked by mystical unpretentiousness and bordering on playful romance. There was so much spontaneity in the moment that it seemed to blur the lines between real and virtual. The two weren't quite aware of what was happening; all they knew was that they just wanted to be with each other.

Meanwhile, one of Dhruv's troupe members came to the scene and informed him about her. 'She has come all the way from Switzerland to shoot a documentary on Banaras,' he said with pride. Dhruv was intrigued to hear that.

Emma then said, 'And, please, you have to help me with it.'

'Sure! What can I do?' Dhruv extended the courtesy.

'Ok… Research work, scheduling, travel, tourism and, yes, some logistics also,' she rattled off, counting each task on her fingers.

'Woah, woah, that's a tall order,' smiled Dhruv.

'I am not done. Above all, you have to ensure that I have a really good time,' she smiled.

Dhruv smiled and stood there marvelling at how lovingly Emma demanded things from him even though they had met barely a few minutes back. Her warmth, enthusiasm and sense of familiarity had begun to mesmerise Dhruv.

'Alright Miss Emma, brace yourself and get ready to soak in the mysticism of this city and I promise you that one day you'll tell me that coming to Banaras was the best decision of your life,' said Dhruv with a sparkle in his eye and an exuberance in his voice as the two of them set out to explore the city.

'Okay, so, of all the places in the world, why did you choose Banaras for your documentary? What got you here?' asked Dhruv, munching an indigenous Banarasi spice-mix. He offered some to Emma.

'Maybe some past karma,' she said softly, with a child-like laugh. It was music to Dhruv's ears.

'You are already high on the mystique of Banaras,' he smiled.

'Don't mind getting totally intoxicated,' she replied playfully. 'I am a student of international relations in Switzerland. As part of my final project, I chose to make a documentary on Banaras.'

'Hmm…interesting… Of all places, you chose India and then Banaras, I'm surprised,' said Dhruv.

'Well, the Swiss Embassy here in India is where I hope to get a job someday,' she said with a twinkle in her eye.

'And what do you love about India?' he asked, looking her in the eye.

'Everything,' she winked, smiling radiantly.

Dhruv was literally glued to her words, her gestures, her eye movements as she said, 'It's a land of a billion stories, each unique and yet bound by a common destiny.'

'Woah, that's some description,' said Dhruv, quite impressed with Emma's fascination for India.

'I guess your company is beginning to show some magic already. I am turning into a wordsmith.'

'Well, trust me, we are just getting started.'

'Alright,' she cheerfully smiled with anticipation and caught Dhruv's extended hand to climb over the ridge as the two started descending down the steps of Assi Ghat.

Chapter 4

The City of Light

'Sweet mother of all that is good and pure!' Emma exclaimed, awestruck by the enormity and variance of the populace present at the Assi Ghat. 'Is there something special today?' she inquisitively enquired.

'Just another day in Kashi,' Dhruv said.

Every conceivable hue of colour was present amongst the people at the Assi Ghat. Some dazzled Emma by their unassuming candour, some enchanted her by their gay abandon, whereas some others won her heart by their uncluttered simplicity. The tea vendors, the balloon sellers, playful children—all of it was cinematically unfolding before her eyes, only to be embellished by a melodious flute playing by the ghat. Emma looked towards the flute player; he seemed to be a middle-aged man with limited means. However, the calm on his face was priceless. He looked towards Emma with a radiant smile. It was a smile that said more than a thousand words. Or maybe it was the peace he experienced in his music that was worth more than the wealth of the richest man around. As the flute player continued, a couple of young boys dressed in traditional attire, began humming a folk song—'Kashi resides in our hearts...'

'What's Kashi?' enquired Emma.

'It's the original name for Banaras, mentioned in our

ancient scriptures.' Dhruv's words blended with the soothing music as he continued, 'Kashi means the city of light.'

Emma's curiosity was escalating by the second, as the melodious flute notes seamlessly blended with her inner orchestration of thoughts, passion and spirit.

A soothing flute player, exuberant kids throwing caution to the winds and a rainbow populace bustling with energy and aspirations—Emma seemed to be in the middle of an abstract poetry in motion.

'Dhruv, isn't this the canvas of life?' she romanticized, referring to Dhruv's recently concluded play by the same name. Dhruv loved the way Emma got philosophical. He sat down on one of the steps and pointing towards the surroundings, said, 'Well, I would say, there is something amiss here.'

'What's that?' she asked.

'Glory' was Dhruv's resolute reply, stemming from the aspirational convictions of his life.

'Maybe there is something beyond glory as well,' reasoned Emma. Her eyes sparkled every time; her words exuded passion.

'And what could that be?' Dhruv wondered aloud.

'Fulfilment,' enunciated Emma with a prophetic twang.

'Well, glory is the means to fulfilment,' smiled Dhruv.

'And what if fulfilment is the means to glory?' Emma smiled. 'What if glory is just a footnote or, at best, a milestone in the long journey of life?' she elaborated.

'Well then, I'd wish for the journey of life to be replete with these milestones and have an indelible stamp of glory,' Dhruv replied.

'That's not in your hand, Dhruv. How your journey is going to unfold is beyond you,' reasoned Emma. 'Dhruv, you

The City of Light

know, when I came backstage today after your play, there was a lot that I wanted to tell you,' she continued.

'As in?' Dhruv curiously enquired.

With a twinkle in her eye, she warmly held his hand and said, 'You are a rare artist. Your work is beyond approval, validation, applause or rejection; it has a touch of divinity and you're a shining star, Dhruv.'

'Well that's what my name means,' said Dhruv, blushing and happily accepting the towering compliment.

'Your name?' she wondered.

'Yes, "Dhruv" means a shining star. In fact, it means the star that shines the brightest. It stands for glory.'

'I see... Now I understand why you are bent towards glory in life,' she wondered aloud.

'Maybe, but by the way, what does "Emma" mean?' Dhruv asked, as the winds along the ghat grew stronger.

Emma, tying her blonde hair in a bun, replied, 'It means fulfilment.'

Dhruv wondered at her words, as the gong of a bell in a nearby temple became the symbolic exclamation to their enriching discussion. 'Glory or fulfilment,' Dhruv smiled at the connotation of their names. It was pure poetry that their respective names also summed up their aspirations in life. The two walked along silently for a second, perhaps still lost in thought. After a moment of silence, Dhruv uttered a word—'Love'—perhaps inviting Emma to articulate her take on it.

Emma smiled and said, 'The glowing flame, steady and eternal.' She expressed this with a fulfilling smile, true to her name.

An impressed Dhruv nodded his head and then articulated his own glory-laced take on love. 'The glorious torch, the inextinguishable fire,' he expressed with magnificence.

'Ambition...' said Emma, inviting Dhruv to express what the word meant to him, as the conversation kept getting richer by the minute.

'Blood, sweat and tears,' came Dhruv's passionate reply, true to his name.

'Contentment,' replied Emma, effortlessly and contrastingly.

'Woah, this is fun,' exclaimed Dhruv. 'My turn now... Success,' he said.

'Smelling the roses,' she romanticized.

Dhruv acknowledged this with a smile and said, 'You know what success is for me? It's there,' Dhruv pointed to the stars up in the sky. 'That's where I want to be; in fact, that's where my mother stays,' he affectionately told her.

Emma was touched to hear that, as she gently patted his head and said, 'You will get there one day, Dhruv.'

The two sat down on the steps of the ghat as the timeless moment gradually seeped into the realm of time. Looking towards the skies, Dhruv said, 'That's my destination. Where is yours?'

Emma placed a hand on her heart and said, 'Right here, that's where I want to be, in everyone's heart.' Dhruv looked on, amazed at Emma's buoyant attitude towards life.

'You know what...' He mischievously glanced at her.

'What?' she said.

'You see that temple right there behind the coconut trees?' pointed out Dhruv.

'I do,' she said, with an element of anticipation.

'Well then, put your racing shoes on and beat me to the temple,' he said.

'Wait a second...wait a sec... Are you kidding?' said

Emma, laughing. And before Dhruv could fathom any further, she started running to get an early advantage.

'What! This isn't fair!' Dhruv too began running.

The two ran with gay abandon, laughing and teasing each other along the way. The air was filled with laughter, merriment and a positive energy as a bunch of overjoyed children too started running with them.

The onlookers and the narrow lanes mattered little to Dhruv and Emma. Perhaps for Dhruv it had been a long time since he had relived his childhood days. Emma's handycam was their third companion through the Banaras sojourn. It captured the raw exuberance of the place, as the two moved along towards the Tulsi Ghat.

Dhruv got a couple of round leaves wrapped around what seemed to Emma to be a mixture of spices. 'What's this?' she asked, trying to decipher.

'This is the elixir of life. It's called "paan". The famous Banaras Paan,' he said proudly.

'Ok, let me try this then,' Emma apprehensively yet excitedly placed the entire thing in her mouth. It was so full of the paan that she couldn't even make a sound. However, her large, expressive green eyes did the talking. The sparkle in them, her dilated pupils and the miniscule yet palpable movement of her eyelashes suggested that she loved the paan.

'Holy cow, it really is the elixir of life!' she exclaimed.

Emma caught the entire paan-making process on her camera, which was building up a rich footage with every passing hour.

Manikarnika Ghat was the next destination. A huge procession of mourners and priests was passing by. Emma switched off her handycam out of sensitivity for the occasion and asked Dhruv, 'Did something happen here?'

'Yes Emma, it's called transformation.'

'Transformation…' repeated Emma.

'That's right. In fact, it's the mother of all transformations; some call it death,' he said.

Emma didn't know how to react as she just nodded, struck by life's harshest reality for a second.

'The Manikarnika Ghat is known as the burning ghat, Emma.' Dhruv's voice was barely audible amidst the loud Vedic chants and invocations of the Almighty. 'We believe that the bodies cremated along the holy Ganges have a chance of attaining moksha, the true liberation from the cycle of birth and death.' Emma was drawn to the spiritual allure of the ghat, which seemed like a melting pot of the various philosophies of life.

'There must be more that's needed to attain moksha,' she inquisitively asked him.

'Absolutely, I think it must be the fulfilment of your purpose in life. Only that perhaps can ascertain moksha,' he wondered aloud, looking closely at the cremation process unfolding at a mile's distance from him.

'You mean, if one dies with an unfulfilled dream, then he or she is reborn until their wishes are fulfilled?' she said.

'Yes,' said Dhruv, after a long pause. Dhruv was totally immersed in the proceedings. His listless yet absorbing stare worried Emma. There was a lot going on inside Dhruv's mind.

'Are you alright?' asked a concerned Emma.

Dhruv didn't respond for a minute, after which he said, 'They tell me, my mother was cremated here. You know

Emma, my mother left on the day I was born.'

Emma was heartbroken to hear that. However, putting on a courageous front, she said, 'Wonder how she'd be boasting about you in the heavens.'

Dhruv smiled and said, 'I hope so. Baba—my father—he tells me that she always wanted her child to be a good, brave human being.'

'I guess that's a standard with mothers across the globe,' said Emma, rather affectionately.

'Really? Is that what your mother also says?' asked Dhruv.

Emma smiled and with a hint of pathos in her voice, she said, 'I don't know.'

Surprised by her reply, Dhruv asked, 'Why?'

'Well, because I don't know who my mother is and neither do I know about my father.'

Dhruv was too dumbstruck to even comment as he patiently heard her.

'I was abandoned by my parents at birth, they say. So I grew up in an orphanage in Zurich,' she said.

'I am so sorry Emma.'

'Not at all,' she said. 'Why should you be? I am not.'

'Earlier, I used to think that I am the abandoned one, but looking at the gift of life and this beautiful universe, I feel that I am the chosen one,' she said with a pleasant smile that spread so much joy that any amount of grief would pale in comparison.

Dhruv was struck by the sheer magnanimity of the young girl. She didn't have an iota of retributive feeling against those who had abandoned her at birth. He looked at Emma with wonderment and hugged her gently out of respect towards her zest for life, as a teary-eyed Emma smiled.

'You're beautiful, Emma,' whispered Dhruv, holding her hand. 'You're beautiful in every way,' he reiterated with greater purpose, as he kissed her right eye. It was a gesture as organic as it was spontaneous. For a while, the two just remained absorbed in the silence of the moment. It was intense.

The evening had set in and the star-studded sky above added to the magnificence of the ambience.

'So, the next title of my play is going to be "Hey Are You Single?"', Dhruv playfully asked.

Emma smiled and said, 'Great! Maybe the title should be "Yes and No".' The playful banter continued in the guise of suggesting play titles.

'On second thoughts, it could also be "The Green-eyed Swiss Wonder",' he grinned.

Emma tried hard to hold back her smile. 'It can also be "In Your Dreams".' She lovingly snubbed him every time.

Dhruv stopped in his tracks and said, 'Could it be "Waltz with the Princess"?' He extended his hand, which she gracefully accepted. She said, 'The Sound of Music.'

He whispered, 'The Silent Whisper.'

And then they danced along as Dhruv's symbolic 'Waltz with the Princess' continued. There was no sound of music, but the whispers of their beating hearts made up for it.

Dhruv and Emma kept meeting for the next three days. Together they experienced the aura of Kashi. Their days would pass in an instant, on the wings of youthful exuberance flying through the sky of romance. Every evening, after they would retire for the day, it felt like someone had turned a gigantic hourglass. Their gaze would remain fixed on the trickling sand, and with every grain of sand, their wait for the first rays of the sun the next morning would only increase.

On the last day of Emma's visit, the two went over to the Dashashwamedha Ghat.

'Good Lord!' exclaimed Emma, totally awestruck by the scale of the ghat, which was being prepped for the famous Ganga Aarti. The reverberating sound of temple bells seemed like a prelude to the main Aarti, as Emma struggled to pronounce 'Dashashwamedha'.

'Legend says that Lord Brahma, God of creation himself, set up these ghats to welcome Lord Shiva, the destroyer of evil,' explained Dhruv. Emma listened intently as he continued, 'The holy Ganges is sacred to us. They say it's a celestial river, which originated from the tresses of Lord Shiva.'

Emma's fascination grew by every second, as she continued questioning. 'So Dhruv, who actually was The One—was it Lord Brahma or Lord Vishnu or Lord Shiva?'

Dhruv smiled at her naivety and said, 'Well, we believe they are all manifestations of the Almighty. You see, Emma, we believe that the infiniteness of the Almighty can be expressed and revered in infinite ways. Some see him as Brahma, the creator, some see him as the charming Lord Krishna, who gave us the message of life, and then some see him as Lord Shiva, who consumed all the pain and poison just so universal righteousness could be upheld. For us, Truth is one and we express it in different ways.'

'Wow!' exclaimed Emma. 'It's a treasure trove of knowledge,' she said. The sound of the temple bells was followed by the loud awakening conches, signalling the commencement of the ceremonies. A troupe of performers had been singing various devotional songs, complementing the conches. The Vedic chants and almighty invocations, though difficult to comprehend, had an exhilarating impact on the listeners. Emma felt a deep urge within. *What was this urge for?* She didn't quite know but it had a sacred connotation for sure. Her mind, her thoughts, all felt divinely energized as the soothing chants kept soaring to unfathomable levels. Huge multi-tiered brass stands carrying earthen lamps were circled majestically in a clockwise manner. The glow of magnificence was almost as if the sun had arisen again on the Dashashwamedha Ghat. Soon, the people along the ghat began offering lamps to the river.

Dhruv whispered in Emma's ear, 'Emma, this is the time one offers a lamp to the holy Ganges. Look around and look within and pray for that one wish of your life to be fulfilled. Mother Ganga doesn't disappoint, they say.'

Emma closed her eyes, but she could still sense the glowing magnificence of the lamps. She looked within and a calm smile adorned her lips. She had nothing to wish for; all she had was gratitude for the gift of life. However, the urge in her heart continued and the reason behind it continued eluding her. She then opened her eyes and saw a visual that would remain etched in her mind for a long time. A thousand lamps on the holy Ganges against a star-studded sky appeared like streaks of burning phosphorus, and amidst their glow and radiance, she saw Dhruv lost in prayer. Pure, silent and intense, Dhruv's prayer seemed like a divine discourse between the Almighty and His chosen one. Emma closed her eyes again and wished for the fulfilment of his dreams.

Emma and Dhruv were sitting at an edit studio where Emma was closely checking out the material she had shot. 'So you

The City of Light

got all you wanted?' asked Dhruv. Perhaps the question had a philosophical connotation.

Emma thought for a second and said, 'Yes, I think I've got everything that I wanted, though I wish I could carry some part of it with me to Mumbai.'

'So you're in Mumbai for the entire summer?' he asked.

'Yes, I'm there till the end of my internship and once that's done, I will go back to Switzerland... By the way, how is your father doing now?' she asked.

'He is much better. The herbal treatment of late has done wonders,' he said.

'Thank God!' she said, and also wrapped up the final edit of her shoot. 'I am done... And Dhruv, thank you so much for making me see Banaras in a way I could've never thought of or managed on my own.'

'You're welcome,' he said.

'Dhruv, I was just thinking... Why don't you come to Mumbai?'

'Me?' he asked

'Yes!' she exclaimed. 'You're such a blessed storyteller and I know a lot of film-makers. You should come over and meet them.'

Dhruv didn't make much of it initially. However, with every passing second, the idea grew on him.

'You see, Dhruv, your final exams will get over next week. After that you can definitely come over to Mumbai.'

'I can't Emma, I just can't leave Baba,' he said.

'You don't need to leave him, Dhruv. You can come over for a few weeks maybe. Who knows, someone might want to bring your story or idea to fruition.'

Dhruv's mind was oscillating between pragmatism and

fantasy. 'I will give it a thought,' he muttered.

'Great… and by the way, I'm leaving tomorrow morning,' she said, packing her camcorder.

The words hit Dhruv pretty hard, though he managed to cover it with a smile. Emma too avoided eye contact and was seemingly focussed on packing her belongings.

'So, finally I will be able to focus on my work from tomorrow,' he said teasingly.

'That's right Dhruv, nobody is going to trouble you anymore,' she agreed.

'Absolutely, nobody is going to cheat me in a race to the coconut tree,' he said.

'That wasn't cheating, I just started early,' she answered.

'Oh please!' said Dhruv in a playful manner. 'In fact, from tomorrow, nobody is going to argue with me about what's important—glory or fulfilment,' he continued with a smile, though the pain in his voice kept becoming more and more apparent with every word he uttered. 'Nobody is going to ask me who is more prominent out of Lord Vishnu, Shiva and Brahma… And nobody is going to tell me the divine truth that there is no bigger gift in life than life itself… Nobody…' he whispered with sacred intensity.

Emma silently looked towards him. She didn't know whether to express herself through her tears or her words, and wondered which one would outweigh the other. Emma gave into the rush and hugged him tightly. 'Come to Mumbai, Dhruv.'

'I am going to miss you, Emma,' he said. The two hugged each other and bid goodbye, but with a promise to meet again.

Chapter 5

The City that Never Sleeps

Emma left for Mumbai the next day. Dhruv's life was back to its mundane state. One such day, Dhruv sat by Ram's side and as was their daily ritual, the two spoke at length over a cup of tea. Sipping his favourite cardamom brew, Ram said, 'Dhruv, what do you plan to do after your finals?'

'Haven't thought much, Baba.'

'I don't see a great future for you here in Banaras. Look, you have to understand that I'm alright and I can take care of myself,' he asserted.

Dhruv nodded and said, 'I know that, Baba, but still I might just join you at work.'

'What nonsense are you talking, Dhruv! I don't need you to join me. I've partnered with a corporate in Delhi and if all goes well, our gems and stones would enter big markets.'

Dhruv didn't speak much, though his perplexed state of mind was apparent in his lost eyes. Ram then gently ruffled his hair and said, 'Don't worry; I will pay off all my debts this summer. This partnership is going to do wonders for us and I am also doing a lot better. You go your way son,' he smiled.

Dhruv kissed his father's hand and said, 'Baba, for me you are the most precious thing in the world. Nothing else matters beyond that.'

'Fine, but now that I am better, you can go to Mumbai for a few weeks and see how things shape up,' he ordered.

'But Baba...'

'No more questions Dhruv, time for you to go to sleep.'

The two smiled as they nostalgically remembered how little Dhruv's endless string of questions would only halt when his father lovingly ordered him to go to sleep.

After much thought and deliberation over the next two weeks, as the final exams got over, Dhruv decided to take the big leap. He spent the last two weeks crystallizing a story that he believed had the potential to enthral one and all. Like all his stories, it had a philosophical slant at its core. However, his storytelling style was entertaining. He decided to give a shot to his 'dream'—a word best personified by the enigma of Mumbai. Dhruv believed that the canvas of his story merited a filmic rendition.

From the mystic bylanes of Banaras to the illusory razzmatazz of Mumbai, Dhruv embarked on a quest for glory. Emma was the only person he knew in that city. The very prospect of meeting her ensured that he was in high spirits all through the twenty-eight hour-long train journey. It was all happening very fast and he felt Lady Luck surely had something up her sleeve.

Emma was elated to see Dhruv. She warmly hugged him at the Mumbai Central Station and said, 'I can't tell you how good it is to see you.'

Dhruv didn't let go of her for a minute. He just stood there silently. Even a wordsmith like him fell woefully short of words. 'I missed...I missed you,' he repeated, his eyes closed and his arms wrapped around her.

'Dhruv, sleep well today because tomorrow is going to be a long day,' she said.

Dhruv's resolute nod meant he was ready to face the music.

The next day, Dhruv accompanied Emma to a suburban film studio situated on the outskirts of an island.

'Dhruv, you've heard about Zubin Mistry?' she asked, as the two entered a yellow-black taxi.

'Zubin Mistry—the maverick film-maker?' he asked

'That's right. He is my internship project mentor,' she confirmed. 'We will be meeting him at the studio, where he is shooting some patchwork for his next film.'

'Woah, okay I really like his work. This must've been a great experience for you,' he said.

'Yes, sort of...but drop your preconceived notions about these people. They are erratic, unpredictable and I am just an intern here for some time,' she said. 'You're ready with your script?' she confirmed.

'Yes I am,' he nodded with a sense of nervous excitement.

'I can't wait to hear it,' said Emma.

Dhruv had written a script on an idea that he held extremely close to his heart. As the taxi entered the studio, it seemed as if they had arrived at a different planet in some other galaxy. The humans there were not just an amalgam of flesh and blood but of dreams, passions and an insurmountable energy. It wasn't all positive, yet it was enchantingly seductive. There were assistants, extras, light-men, spot boys—all consumed by their tasks. A huge set was being put in place as technicians and facilitators helped in setting up the props and the gadgetry. The frantic speed at which things were unfolding on the set was perhaps second only to the feverish pace of events in Dhruv's life at that moment. For a minute, Dhruv was overawed by the enormity and scale of the opulence. It was a world of make-belief; intoxicating and addictive, yet so real.

Barely had the gravity of the moment and the occasion sunk in when Dhruv received a rude shock from the team of assistants who pushed him aside as the maverick Zubin Mistry made his way to the set. Unkempt hair, a dishevelled beard, and an extravagant and rather snobbish swagger made the man stand out. Only a few seconds had passed when he hurled a mouthful of abuses at his assistants, who he believed weren't up to the mark. The shrill admonishment by the film-maker unnerved a young Dhruv, who was barely a few steps away from him. Zubin's cold stare caught Dhruv's rather lost gaze. Dhruv gingerly bowed and tried to greet him. However, Zubin just went past him as if Dhruv was some obscure entity.

The entire day passed but Dhruv could not muster the courage to walk up to Zubin and give him Emma's reference.

'So, you couldn't get hold of him for even a second in an eighteen-hour shift?' Emma enquired.

'Yes, I mean the man just didn't seem receptive.' Dhruv gulped down a morsel of food.

'Dhruv, it's a crazy place. These people don't have any regard for anything. You will have to somehow hold his attention and get him to listen to you.'

Dhruv nodded and started thinking about how he would

approach Zubin the next day.

The next few days were a lesson in patience for young Dhruv. Zubin didn't meet him for ten days on the trot. However, Dhruv wasn't one of those who would throw in the towel that easily. On the eleventh day, Dhruv decided to bite the bullet, come what may. In between two shots, he mustered the courage and went straight to Zubin.

'Sir, I am Dhruv Samrat,' he confidently introduced himself, extending his hand only to be rudely snubbed by a cold stare. Dhruv's smile, however, didn't waver. 'Emma Schellenberg, the Swiss student, must have had a word…' Before Dhruv could even complete, Zubin started shouting hysterically at an assistant standing far away. 'Bloody scoundrel, how many times do I have to tell you the lighting pattern!' he snarled with ferocity. Dhruv quietly made way for a fuelled Zubin who charged towards the assistant.

Emma was also a part of the crew. However, beyond a point, even she couldn't pester Zubin to hear Dhruv's narration. For Dhruv, every passing day brought with it the glaring realities of the illusory world they called Bollywood, where meeting people and getting their attention even for a minute—despite there being many brokers and middlemen who promised a ten-minute window in return for a quick buck—was akin to an Everest climb.

However, the next day, a desperate Dhruv sprung a surprise out of nowhere. Zubin was relaxing on his chair with his legs crossed and resting on top of another chair in front of him. Dhruv's vigilant eyes sensed an opportunity and he rushed towards him. The sound of Dhruv's racing steps had barely reached Zubin and his rolled-up tongue was just about to hit his palate, when Zubin signalled him to leave.

'Phew...' said Zubin, as Dhruv turned back.

However, a couple of steps later, Dhruv turned back again towards Zubin. Zubin looked at him with disdain; but Dhruv didn't budge an inch this time.

'Don't you understand that you are not wanted right now? Come later,' he blasted him. Heads turned around and a few asked Dhruv to leave immediately. An unnerved Dhruv, however, stood his ground and said, 'I need fifteen minutes of your time, that's it. I'll not ask for a minute more.' An assistant came towards him to guide him out. However he kept reiterating, 'Just fifteen minutes of your patience.' Dhruv was escorted out by the assistant who gave him a word of advice. 'Listen, we have hundreds like you who come up here every day. Zubin can't be giving his fifteen minutes to everyone. We have a job to do and film to make, you get that?'

Dhruv smiled at him and said, 'No I don't get that because I am not one of the hundreds who come here every day. I came here not because I am enticed by the razzmatazz of this industry. I came here because I have a good story to tell. That's it... Period!'

Dhruv's conviction resonated in every word he uttered, as he walked out of the studio.

Far away from the superfluous extravagance of the glamour world, Dhruv and Emma were enjoying a local Mumbai street delicacy at Nariman Point.

The gorgeous rays of the setting sun had a thousand stories to tell, even though ironically Mumbai had always been synonymous with the rising sun.

'I'll be leaving tomorrow,' he said with a sense of

despondency coupled with disgust.

'I'm so sorry for calling you. I had no idea that Zubin would not even meet you,' she said regretfully.

Dhruv looked around Nariman Point, which had always been fabled as the microcosm of the great Mumbai dream. The exhilaration of the sea waves seemed second only to Dhruv's quest and passion. The hard rocks on which the two were perched bore testimony to Dhruv's rugged journey. And amidst all the pursuits, blossomed a romance, pure and heartwarming.

'Emma...' he whispered.

'Yes, Mr Give-me-fifteen-minutes?' she smiled. The two had a hearty laugh till their sides started aching.

'Well, it was a pretty emotive appeal, wasn't it? And this Zubin Mistry still didn't even give me fifteen square minutes,' his laughter continued. 'But you know what Emma? I have never ever been so pumped up to go after my dreams. Never...' he said with renewed zeal.

'Dhruv, I guess that's the Mumbai charm talking here.'

Dhruv just smiled, trying to make sense of the wondrous place called Mumbai.

'But how are you going to break this wall and get to Mr Zubin?' asked Emma.

A thousand thoughts and ideas were popping up in Dhruv's mind. Some were plain noisy, others had a musical rhythm; however, the background chorus resonated with the never-give-up creed that Dhruv so firmly believed in.

'I am coming back, Emma,' he assured her, warmly holding her hand and playfully winking. 'Maybe, it's not the Mumbai charm that's keeping me going, it might just be someone else's charm,' he teased, setting the ball rolling.

'Okay, I guess that "someone" must be really special,' she smiled.

'Yes she is. Only thing is that she cheats when competing in a race.'

Emma squinted at him with annoyance. However, even her purported anger had an enduring innocence.

'She won that race, fair and square,' Emma asserted, getting up in a rush of adrenaline.

'Well that's what they say after using unfair means,' he said.

'Unfair? Fine, let's have it again,' Emma said. 'You see that coffee shop behind the pole?'

'Oh I do,' he replied.

'Brace up, big boy, because you are on your way to a second defeat.'

Dhruv smiled and nodded. He was always elated to see Emma in a fiercely competitive mood. On the count of three, the two ran, throwing caution to the winds. Overcome with laughter and unbridled joy, they ran as if they had looted a fortune, though ironically even a fortune would pale in comparison to the priceless moments they experienced together.

Like the first race, Dhruv lost again. However, the one contest Dhruv just wasn't ready to lose was getting across to Zubin Mistry and making him hear his script.

Back in Banaras, Dhruv began contemplating ways to make an impact on Zubin Mistry.

'Baba, what should I do to make this man at least hear me out?' wondered Dhruv aloud.

The City that Never Sleeps

'You know Dhruv, there is an old saying in our trade—if your customer is blind, make him hear, if he is deaf, make him see and if he is both, make him feel,' said Ram as he leaned back on his chair. 'Your customer seems both deaf and blind. You've got a hard walk up the road kid,' he said with an endearing smile adorned with wrinkles, or as Ram eloquently put it—'lines of wisdom'.

Dhruv quietly listened. His innocent nod and large, expressive eyes always managed to get a loving pat on the head from Ram. For Ram, he was always his little inquisitive child, destined for greatness.

Dhruv was happy to see Ram's progress with regards to his health even though he would experience bouts of incessant coughing occasionally.

Ram's words—'make him feel'—stuck with Dhruv, who met with his theatrical troupe. Many of his former colleagues had left the city in search of greener pastures. Some of them occasionally met and performed purely for recreational purposes. Dhruv, however, was toying with an idea, which seemed outlandish yet doable.

'Guys, I need a favour from you,' Dhruv addressed his former teammates backstage, near the green room where they'd sit and brainstorm for hours together. 'I need your help today.'

A general murmur spread across the room. 'I have written a story, which is too long for a stage play and rightly deserves a rendition on the silver screen. However, I need to entice this film-maker into the world of my story. We need to blow him away with something that stirs his soul.' Dhruv's passion was seeping through every pore of his body.

'But Dhruv, as you said, your story cannot be a stage play,' one of the troupe members pointed out.

'Yes, but we could do an introductory skit...or...or some innovative visualization...and that could get him hooked,' Dhruv's bubbling ideas made him fumble for words.

'We're not hookers, Dhruv. We are artists,' said another on a slightly dismal note.

'I agree,' Dhruv calmly said. 'Which is why I said, "I need a favour".'

'So will he come to Banaras?' asked another one.

'No,' Dhruv hesitatingly said. 'We'll have to go to Mumbai,' said Dhruv, dropping the bombshell.

Before the murmur got really loud, Dhruv said, 'With whatever little savings I have, I will pay for your fare. Also I promise to take you all out to the film studio, but I really need this one from you all.'

There was dead silence in the room. The only thing audible was Dhruv's loud breath laced with passion and anticipation. The man was desperate to be heard in a glamour-drunk world where artistic whispers rarely overpowered the din of the cash-rich.

One of the troupe members then spoke up, 'Dhruv, you remember our play, The Canvas of Life?'

'Of course, I do. We worked hard for that and our convictions really paid off,' Dhruv replied.

'Yes, right, it did pay off, but I also remember the day each one of us rubbished your idea the first time you narrated it. We said that it's never going to work, people would not connect with it.'

Dhruv kept smiling, as his friend continued, 'A couple of days later, Dhruv, it hit us like a thunderbolt. It was slow intoxication and it just kept growing on us. That's the thing about your craft Dhruv, it has a connection with the Lord above.'

Dhruv had a lump in his throat, as he soaked in each word that his friend was saying.

'So today, we're going to do this not because you're taking us to a film studio or because you are paying our fare but because we believe that your craft deserves its rightful place in the universe,' he asserted with a sense of purpose, which was seconded by all other troupe members.

Dhruv hugged him and with genuine gratitude, whispered, 'Thanks.'

The troupe worked hard on a high-impact skit, which would serve as a prelude to Dhruv's narration. Emma still had a few days left in her internship stint under Zubin Mistry.

After a few days of intense preparations, the troupe was ready as they packed the props and other material required for the skit. Dhruv was all set to visit Mumbai again. It was an early morning train from Banaras to Mumbai. He didn't sleep too well the night before. The butterflies in his stomach were understandable, but what had disturbed him alarmingly was a premonition he had about something untoward and unholy. His fear seemed unfounded. However, something didn't seem right to him.

'Baba, I have this strange feeling that I just can't describe,' he said, zipping his bag, which was kept on the floor.

Ram lovingly smiled at him and opening a drawer by the bedside, he said, 'Come here.'

Dhruv inquisitively got up from the floor and went towards him. Ram took out a granite-red stone from the drawer and slid it along a thread. He then gently tied the locket around his son's neck.

'Son, this stone is considered an auspicious one in our family of alchemists. Legend has it that your grandfather, after years of penance and perseverance, crafted this masterpiece.'

'Baba, I've always wanted to know about the priest's prophecy. Didn't he say that I'm going to be an alchemist one day?' he asked. Ram smiled and nodded, 'He did say that, but prophecies don't govern our actions.'

'Is alchemy real, Baba?' Did our forefathers really know the magic of transforming lead into gold?'

Ram kissed his son on his forehead and said, 'You'll know that one day, Dhruv. It's a journey that you have to undertake.' Dhruv had a couple of more questions as usual; however, Ram very affectionately said, 'No more questions Dhruv, time to go and…'

'And?' asked Dhruv.

'And discover your destiny,' his father said almost prophetically.

Dhruv smiled as his starry-eyed face lit up with dreams and anticipation, as he began yet another tryst with the city of Mumbai.

Chapter 6

The Most Successful Failure

*D*hruv and his troupe members reached Mumbai in the wee hours of the morning. Dhruv was well aware that the entire effort could go in vain if Zubin Mistry didn't turn up for their skit. Emma was stunned by their marathon effort, as she exclaimed, 'I can't believe the fact that you guys have worked out a skit, especially for this.'

'Well, we have and now it's up to you to make sure Zubin at least sees what we wish to offer,' explained Dhruv, as his team members were still awestruck by the opulence of the film set.

'Last time around, he got really mad at you,' Emma reminded him.

Dhruv seemed hungry and poised to make an impact. His intensity was palpable.

Emma tried calming him down and said, 'Relax, take a deep breath. I will try and get him to the floor right behind the one we are shooting on at the moment'.

'You mean, Floor IX?' confirmed Dhruv.

'That's right. I checked up the schedules and found out that Floor IX is unoccupied for the entire evening,' said Emma, as her heavy breath conveyed her anxiety.

'You guys, set up the props. Feel free to use the audio-video equipment there and just give a knockout narration,' she said, hesitantly smiling as a part of her mind had begun devising a plan to bring Zubin Mistry on Floor IX.

'Alright, thanks!' Dhruv hurriedly hugged her and with a couple of claps, he energized his group as they made their way to Floor IX, which was unoccupied and unattended. Courtesy Emma's presence, the attendants there allowed Dhruv and his troupe to set up their equipment and use the audio-video apparatus present there.

Emma knew that any failed attempt from Dhruv would not only dampen his spirits but also dent her own equation with Zubin Mistry. However, she did bite the bullet and she walked up to him, as he was waiting for the shot to be set up.

'Sir, if you don't mind, can I suggest something?' she said softly.

'Yes, tell me,' came his characteristic deadpan reply.

'Sir, I think we can set up a small crew on another floor for shooting patchwork and fillers,' she suggested, trying hard to get him to Floor IX.

True to his eccentricity, Zubin didn't nod or utter a word. However, something struck him, and courtesy some divine intervention, he started walking towards Floor IX to evaluate. Emma quickly joined him. With butterflies in her stomach and a prayer on her lips, Emma wished well for Dhruv. As the two entered the main lobby surrounding the stage, Emma's eyes were feverishly browsing the floor, trying to catch a glimpse of Dhruv and his troupe. And then out of nowhere, a symphony started playing. It was an enigmatic tune, and what followed was a compelling voiceover. The visualizations produced by the actors corresponding to the voiceover were breathtaking. The silhouettes on the projector screen swayed to the rhythm and tempo of Dhruv's narrative. Zubin wondered what was happening and was too stunned to react. However, he had surely stopped in his tracks to catch a glimpse of something extraordinary yet simple unfolding before his eyes.

'This is the story of the most successful failure ever,' said the voiceover.

The paradoxical phrase, 'successful failure,' struck a chord with Zubin. Then, Dhruv came out in the open and started narrating the story amidst subtle background music and a theatrical performance by his troupe. The story was a gut-wrenching portrayal of a young man who was destined for greatness; however, greatness came at a price. Dhruv trembled with emotion, his lips quivered with intensity; his expression was so impeccably divine that it seemed as if the Gods themselves had descended to the floor.

Zubin and Emma sat down and so did a dozen more, who had come looking for Zubin.

It wasn't a play, it wasn't a movie; it was just one man's passionate narration of a story he wished to see on celluloid one day.

Emma just couldn't stop smiling. She was extremely proud of Dhruv. Her eyes kept switching between watching Dhruv's play and the expressions on Zubin's face.

The floor managers of the studio couldn't quite fathom what was going on. However, the technicalities of permissions and clearances were too trivial compared to the divinity unfolding before them. They couldn't muster the courage to stop Dhruv and his crew.

Dhruv continued narrating the journey of his protagonist—Arjun.

'"Success" and "failure", two words that are perhaps more discriminatory than racism; they define a man's life. They're binary modes of the machines we humans have become.'

Everybody was hooked as Dhruv's stirring narration continued.

'Success and failure are two sides of the same coin—the coin we call the theatre of life. And in the theatre of life, success comes at a price, at a sacrifice. Our character pays a price and, honestly, success for him was nothing but moving on from one failure to another, with his heart and soul intact. Perhaps such is the irony of life that success or failure actually depends on the lens through which you're looking at the theatre of life.'

By now, the crowd had broken into a loud applause. The resonant claps added to the spellbinding spectacle as Dhruv seemed lost in deep introspection. His colleagues had, by now, wrapped up their bit, but Dhruv wasn't done.

'Those who touch the skies yearn to have their feet on the ground, and those who are rooted to it, long for wings to fly.'

Placing his right hand on his chin and walking around, he said, 'Why does one want to be a part of this race of dualities—success-failure, victory-defeat, pain-pleasure—I wonder. Perhaps it's all about rising above...rising above the dualities; that perhaps is true liberation. Salvation lies within.'

The sound of the claps had engulfed the floor to a level where the last line was barely audible. In fact, the last few lines weren't scripted or premeditated; perhaps it was an dialogue between Dhruv and his soul. The standing ovation continued for a few minutes as Dhruv stood there smiling and still contemplating what he had just said. Zubin hadn't moved an inch. Much like Dhruv, he was still immersed in the narrative that he had heard. After a couple of minutes, he stood up and true to his eccentric self, he walked up to

Dhruv, looked him in the eye, turned around and shouted out loud to his assistant, 'Ryan, remember the time I told you how genius storytelling is now a thing of the past?'

Ryan nodded in agreement, as Zubin continued, 'Turns out, I was wrong, 'cause genius storytelling is very much alive and breathing right now on stage IX.'

He looked back at Dhruv and said, 'You know why we don't have great stories anymore?'

Dhruv shrugged his shoulders and nervously waited to hear from Zubin.

'That's because some rigid maverick or an old warhorse refuses to give fifteen minutes to somebody who is passionate and hungry enough,' he dramatically announced. 'But then there's someone who doesn't take no for an answer, who doesn't beg around or wait for his moment but instead he gets up and bloody hell, he bulldozes his way in and creates time and space for himself,' said a visibly impressed Zubin.

Dhruv felt bursts of elation deep down, only to be calmed down by the fear of premature jubilation.

Zubin signalled the others to get back to work. After a couple of minutes, he sat down on a bench and asked Dhruv to sit beside him. Then without mincing words, he told him, 'It's the most intense story I've heard in recent times.'

Dhruv thanked him for the kind words, as Zubin continued, 'Loved every bit of it, but I didn't get the last line, when you said—'Salvation lies within'. What was that all about?' he enquired, sipping some tea, which the spot boy had got for both of them.

A contemplative silence had gripped Dhruv. 'Salvation lies within'—he wondered what those words meant and how they were perhaps ingrained in his subconscious.

'Nothing... it probably came from the heart,' said Dhruv rather unassumingly.

A brief silence followed. Perhaps it was a prelude to something extraordinary.

'You have the script ready?' asked Zubin, lighting up a cigarette.

Dhruv excitedly nodded and said, 'Oh absolutely! I have the full version with me.'

Zubin's face lit up on hearing that, as he said, 'Dhruv, time to say hello to the stars.'

Dhruv's heart was pacing like an unleashed racehorse running for pole position. All his dreams, pursuits, flashed before his eyes as he reached out for his bag kept close by. Unzipping it, he took out the draft script titled 'The Theatre of Life'.

'The Theatre of Life,' read out Zubin. 'Interesting title, but I really loved your opening line: "The most successful failure ever". How's that for a title?' he asked.

Dhruv smiled and said, 'Whatever pleases you.'

Zubin smirked and said, 'I always do what pleases me, and you know what, kid? Your life is about to change.' With these words, Zubin took the script and kept it in his handbag. On a parting note, he asked his assistant to line up meetings with Dhruv over the next few days.

Dhruv's joy knew no bounds. The moment Zubin stepped out of the studio, Dhruv heaved a sigh of relief, and cried out loud with happiness. His troupe members too joined him in the euphoria. Dhruv just abandoned all pressures and anxieties for that moment, as he lay down flat on the floor, light and carefree. 'Phew...we did it,' he softly exclaimed as his troupe rallied around him.

Floor IX of that coveted film studio was witness to the commencement of a man's tryst with his destiny. It was chaotic, jubilant and yet so serene. Perhaps that's how success felt.

A wave of excitement swept them as they made their way out of the studio. 'Woohoo! Woohoo! Can we make way for the next big thing—Dhruv Samrat!' shouted his friend amidst claps and whistles as the revelry amongst the group increased by the minute. Dhruv hugged each one of them and thanked them for their unconditional support.

As elated as Dhruv was, he was most of all grateful to the one woman who got him this opportunity. It may have been the hand of destiny or maybe it was the touch of a green-eyed Swiss girl who had set the wheels of change in motion. Emma's tryst with Dhruv's destiny was the stuff romanticism is made of.

'You guys carry on, I will join you later,' Dhruv told his friends, as he waited at the studio for Emma to get over. As the day ripened and eventually dissolved to make way for the evening, Dhruv kept gazing towards the studio hoping to catch a glimpse of his wonder woman, when suddenly he felt a gentle tap on his shoulder.

He turned around. It was Emma. The radiant smile on her lips and the euphoric buoyancy of Dhruv's racing heart culminated in an affectionate hug. It had been an overwhelming moment for him. Perhaps it was the first time that this boy was experiencing some joy in his otherwise chequered life thus far. He softly whispered in Emma's ear, 'Is this all real?'

Emma whispered back in his ear, 'It's a reality in an illusory world.'

Dhruv laughed gently. Emma's words had an uncanny

depth yet innocence, similar to the fabric that Dhruv's inquisitiveness was made of.

'And what are you—a beautiful mirage in the desert of my life or the single greatest reality of my existence?' he asked rather philosophically. His smile camouflaged the intensity of emotions waiting to pour out from his heart.

'I'm just Emma, and "Emma" stands for fulfilment. You remember that?' she asked.

'Of course, I do.'

He then held her hand and said, 'Come along with me.'

'Where?' she asked, puzzled at his exuberance.

Dhruv excitedly took her along. The two ran around laughing with gay abandon, throwing caution to the winds. Restless and full of life, they reached the coveted Floor IX of the studio.

'So you want me to revisit your place of glory for the day? Well Dhruv, just so you know, I was right here,' she affectionately smiled.

'You see that stage, Emma? That's been my universe from ever since I can remember.'

Feeling a rush of adrenaline, Dhruv excitedly went up the stage in a stride. 'Hand on my heart, Emma, whenever I've been here, I've only spoken the truth and nothing else.' Dhruv was breathing heavily. The emotional twang in his voice and the burning intensity of his words meant that he had something deep to say.

'Are you alright, Dhruv?' asked Emma.

'Oh, I've never been more alright, since childhood,' he smiled.

'You remember our first meeting when I just zipped past everyone to speak to you?'

Emma nodded with a smile to convey that she remembered, as she held Dhruv's hand and went up the stage.

'That day, I just knew that I have some cosmic connection with this girl, and if that day, I didn't speak to her, then that one visual of the green-eyed girl would lurk in my mind forever.'

Emma was blushing with excitement as her racing heart continued beating at a rate second only to the adrenaline rush that Dhruv was experiencing.

'Turns out, meeting you didn't help, 'cause the visual of that green-eyed girl is even more deeply etched in my mind. And, you know what? That girl is blushing right now.'

Emma could barely hold back her emotions as she gently kissed Dhruv on his cheek.

Dhruv continued pouring his heart out on what was shaping up to be a memorable day in his life. 'I've always dreamt of being at the centre of the universe, telling a story or connecting with the universe in a way that makes my mother up there (he pointed to the sky) proud of me.'

Dhruv's words were passionately stirring, the kind a craftsman like him would possess in any case, but also arising from the goodness that his heart of gold possessed. He continued, 'But today, I realized that it's not just storytelling or connecting with the audiences that's a part of my universe...'

Dhruv seemed too overwhelmed with emotion to continue. He paused for a second as Emma asked him, 'Are you okay?'

Large, pearl-like tears were clinging to her eyelashes as if held by an olive branch. Her face was adorned by a beautiful smile as Dhruv walked a couple of steps towards her. His deep breaths were in harmonious coordination with the spring in his steps. He was too overwhelmed to speak as he held

Emma's hand and affectionately kissed them.

'Honest to my craft, if this stage be the canvas of my life, you're more precious than the first clap that an artist yearns for. And God is the witness—you're the most cherished reality of my fictitious world. You're my point of absolution,' the craftsman Dhruv was in full flow.

However, the touch of divinity in his words that day was rendered not by his artistic prowess, but by the depth of emotion he felt for Emma, as his head rested affectionately against hers.

Emma whispered, 'Never let go.'

It was a moment when their emotions and love unfurled from the deepest recesses of their souls as the two sealed the moment with a passionate kiss. Etched in the annals of time, it was a moment of catharsis for them. It was perhaps divine ordainment that the moment unfolded right at the centre of the stage, which was a metaphor for the canvas of Dhruv's life. The two were in a different celestial universe—a universe where rainbows were a norm and cloudy skies were an aberration; a universe where happiness was the only currency and one only sought blessings. They were swaying to the tune of their hearts. Leaning against Dhruv's forehead, Emma closed her eyes. It was as if she foresaw her entire life unfold in that second. Dhruv kissed her on her eyes and then…

His phone rang. It was past twelve in the night. The ring didn't have a very pleasant vibe. Dhruv's heart skipped a beat as he hurriedly answered it. It was a call from Banaras. The voice on the other end wasn't too familiar. It was a shaky and incoherent voice, which further compounded Dhruv's anxiety, as he agitatedly asked out loud, 'Is Baba okay?'

Alas! The reply on the other end chilled the marrow within his bones. Emma could sense by his expressions that hell had broken loose somewhere. Dhruv's hands were trembling with fear. He felt numb. His parched throat barely allowed him to speak and his cold feet didn't move an inch. Somehow, he mustered up the courage to say, 'I'm coming.' As he hung up, he started crying piteously. Emma kept asking him, but Dhruv was a sobbing mess. He just wanted to rush home but alas, he was more than a thousand kilometres away from it.

Ram Samrat had suffered a massive heart attack. It was a call from his neighbour who had got him admitted to a nearby hospital. A panic-struck Dhruv was totally paralyzed. A sense of helplessness had gripped him to a point where he started crying out loud for help.

Emma helplessly tried calming him down.

'Baba… Baba…' he shouted. 'Emma, he is all I have.' With these words, he ran out frantically looking for a taxi or some other means of conveyance.

'Dhruv! Dhruv!' Emma followed him outside, but he was uncontrollable.

Emma held him tightly and said, 'Get a hold, Dhruv. Get a hold!' She patted Dhruv's cheeks. 'Dhruv, listen to me, you can't get there by a train before twenty-four hours.'

Dhruv's hands and lips were trembling with anxiety.

'You'll have to take a flight,' she asserted. 'Come…' she said, as the two rushed towards the airport.

It was perhaps one of the longest nights of Dhruv's life. As they reached the airport, Dhruv realized that he didn't have the resources to buy the expensive ticket. Emma pooled in whatever she had at that moment. As much as she wanted to accompany Dhruv to Banaras, the two ran out of cash. Somehow, they managed to gather enough for Dhruv's ticket.

'Dhruv, it'll all be good...' she said, repeatedly patting his shoulder and rubbing his hands.

A flood of negative thoughts had stunned Dhruv. He quietly hugged Emma and without saying a word, moved towards the boarding area. On the flight, a dispirited Dhruv closed his eyes and joined his hands in prayer. His heart sunk every time an untoward thought flashed across his mind. He winced and interlaced his fingers even more tightly in prayer, as the plane soared into the skies in sharp contrast to his sinking heart.

The Most Successful Failure

Chapter 7

The Theatre of Life...and Death

So deep and profound was his prayer for his Baba that he seemed lost in a maze of memories, nostalgia and a deep fear of loss. How he wished he had never left Banaras. How he wished his Baba could be well again. Barely had his abounding wishes and prayers plateaued that the plane landed in Banaras. Dhruv immediately connected with his neighbours and local friends. Breathless with anxiety and running full steam, he reached the intensive care unit of the local Kashi hospital. The sight there was eerily unpleasant. He saw his neighbour, Mr Lal, standing there. He was silent. Dhruv badly wanted to know what had happened. Or maybe a part of him feared to know the unknown.

'How is Baba?' he asked him. His voice was trembling, his forehead and palms were sweating profusely. Dhruv didn't get an answer. Tears had already started rolling down his cheeks and he could feel a lump in his throat. He went up to the doctor and as he entered the ward, he saw his Baba. Dhruv's facial muscles had started drooping under the weight of immense grief. Ram's bare body was ravaged by needles, tubes and an oxygen mask. He was barely moving.

The doctor then walked up to Dhruv, held his hands and said, 'He doesn't have time. All yours,' as his team, one by one, started removing all the tubes from Ram's ailing body and made way for Dhruv.

'No… No…' he cried out. 'This can't be… You have to do something,' he begged.

'You're missing out on precious time, Dhruv,' the doctor asserted.

Copious tears started pouring out of Dhruv's eyes. He cried painfully.

The ascending cries were halted by a small gesture from Ram. He could barely move, but his eyes invited Dhruv to come closer. Dhruv somehow controlled himself and went towards his ailing father, who was getting ready for his departure to another world. Dhruv held his Baba's hand, as Ram smiled. He gently nodded as if asking Dhruv not to cry. Perhaps he wanted to say something but couldn't really muster the strength. The smile didn't leave his lips. Every time Dhruv cried, he nodded and smiled. Perhaps he wanted Dhruv to bid him goodbye with a smiling face.

Dhruv kissed him on his forehead and said, 'Baba, I love you.' He then placed his father's head on his lap. Memories of how his father would cuddle him to sleep flashed across his mind. Alas! It was a painful role reversal. Visuals of how Ram brought him up as a single parent, listening to his endless tales and answering his strangest questions, continued revisiting Dhruv. Ram wore a complacent smile. Perhaps he had held on all this while, waiting for Dhruv's lap.

And then… And then that smile never faded. Ram Samrat was dead.

It was a cold Monday morning when the piles of wood were

being stacked at the Manikarnika Ghat. The burning ghat, as it was called, bore an uncanny resemblance to young Dhruv's inner self. Ashes were all that were left. The holy Ganges seemed calm and serene, as Dhruv, along with his neighbours and friends, gently lowered his father's body wrapped in a white cotton cloth on the funeral pyre.

A local priest shouted rather insensitively, 'Heavy wood on top of the body is important or else the heat will expand the muscles, and the body will arch out'.

Dhruv looked at him. Such was the pain in Dhruv's eyes that it shamed the priest, who now seemed apologetic. *Alas! He was just doing his duty*, thought Dhruv.

As the body was gently placed over the stack of wood, there were tourists hovering around, wood sellers trying to bargain for the best prices, and sandalwood-owners making a sales pitch for their oil to facilitate the burning. Amidst all this, at the centre lay a body, devoid of life. The contrast spoke volumes about the nihilism of the universe. And then it was time for Dhruv to light up the pyre. As he held up the blazing torch in his hand, the priests began chanting a Sanskrit hymn, which meant 'God alone is the Truth'.

Dhruv then realized that he was an orphan.

Chapter 8

Salvation Lies Within

It took Dhruv weeks to come to terms with a loss this deep and irreparable. Emma came over for a few days. Her heart went out to Dhruv. She did comfort him a little with her presence but then Dhruv had a lot on his plate and she too had to fly back to complete her internship. All the family dues, documentations and bank accounts had to be taken care of. As he stepped up for his family business, he realized that things were a far cry from simple and sorted. The late Ram Samrat had taken a huge loan from the bank and other creditors, in a bid to expand his family business of gems and stones. Dhruv hadn't been in the thick of things as far as business matters were concerned. Ram always wanted his son to follow his own pursuits but unfortunately Dhruv had to step in for the family business at a time when he wasn't really prepared.

Amidst all of this, Dhruv received a message from Emma, which said: *Dhruv, my internship is drawing to a close. I know that it's a tough time for you but I just want to let you know that I'm here in Mumbai for only a couple of weeks. Take care.*

Dhruv read the message in the confines of his study room. Scattered on his table was a bunch of account sheets and bills, waiting to be attended to. As Dhruv took a breather and leaned back his head, he saw a folder from the corner of his eye. It was his script, 'The Most Successful Failure,' a copy of which he had given to film-maker Zubin Mistry, a month back.

It was like a whiff of fresh air for Dhruv. Nothing made him calmer than his craft. He realized that he hadn't heard from Zubin for a long time. Dhruv's mind felt like a rudderless ship at the mercy of the winds.

A rather dreamy breeze took his mind to Mumbai where his aspirations and Emma were waiting for the fruition of their prospects. However, turbulent gusts of wind brought him back to the ghats where unfinished business, accounts and debts were demanding his attention. The quintessential dilemmas in his life continued having a field day at the expense of his already bruised mind. He was also missing Emma. Dhruv hadn't been too responsive of late, which was understandable. However, under the layers of grief and responsibility, there was a flame of pure love glowing silently yet majestically, sparks of which were experienced by both Dhruv and Emma on that fateful day in Mumbai. Amidst all this mental turmoil, Dhruv picked up the phone and before he could dial a number, he received a call from Emma herself.

'Dhruv...Dhruv...' she sounded a bit perplexed.

'Emma...Is everything okay?' he asked with concern.

'Dhruv, something is not right here,' she replied with a strange sense of urgency. 'Dhruv, did you speak to Zubin all this while?' she asked.

'I tried calling him two to three times, but he didn't respond. I also sent a couple of messages and mails, but did not get any response from him,' he said.

'Dhruv, he is up to something. I don't know what exactly he is up to, but I don't get a good feeling. You must come down immediately,' she said.

'What are you saying, Emma? I have creditors breathing down my neck. I...I can't,' he said with abounding uneasiness.

In a panic-stricken voice, Emma shrieked, 'Dhruv, I understand that, and trust me, I would have not insisted on you coming. But...but...'

A tongue-tied Emma couldn't speak further. Her studded silence though spoke volumes about the gravity of the situation.

Dhruv sighed. 'I'll try and reach there in a couple of days. Let me see.'

Dhruv couldn't quite fathom what was wrong. Honestly, he had no time to speculate or second-guess. On his attorney's advice, he met the creditors the next day. It was a hands-on lesson in swallowing pride for young Dhruv. The creditors half-heartedly and rather hastily expressed their condolences and rushed to the main point of the meeting.

'Dhruv, your father was a great man, and as a true son, I'm sure you will fulfil all his obligations,' said one of them.

The other one added a religious touch to it and said, 'Our scriptures tell us that the departed soul doesn't rest in peace until all its debts have been paid off.'

One of them was rather brazen. He said, 'Dhruv, I barely knew your father and I want my money back. I should have perhaps guessed by his fragile appearance and chronic cough that lending money to him would land me in trouble.'

Barely had the man finished when Dhruv flipped and caught him by the scuff of his neck. The attorney intervened before it flared up into an all-out brawl. Dhruv was livid. The ill-mouthed creditor continued his tirade. 'You're a bloody defaulter. Back off, you defaulter,' he mumbled, catching his breath. A furious Dhruv eventually stepped back but the damage had been done.

He then calmed down a little, his hands still trembling, as he said, 'Look, I promise each of you that I'm going to pay every single penny of yours.'

'You have no other option. Remember, your house is mortgaged,' lashed out the confrontational creditor, yet again. Dhruv chose to ignore him and reiterated, 'That's a promise, and I say this remembering my late father.'

After a minute of silence, one of them said, 'Fine, but Dhruv, for our assurance, make sure you don't move out of the city.' The other creditors seconded that.

Dhruv pleaded, 'Listen, I have some unfinished work in Mumbai but I'll be back in three to four days. Please, that's the last thing that I'll request.' Dhruv's attorney also pleaded for his case and they somehow managed to pacify them for a few days.

However, for Dhruv, it was a case of jumping out of the devil's mouth, straight into the deep sea, namely the sea of Mumbai.

Emma embraced him tightly as she saw him at the station. However, her body language exuded an unnerving anxiety. Dhruv asked her the reason behind her worry, but she couldn't quite articulate it. Perhaps, she wasn't too sure about what was happening.

'You're still with Zubin?' he asked.

'He released me a couple of weeks before the scheduled completion of my internship. I'm just waiting for the final letter,' she said. 'But lately, he is up to something, Dhruv, and

I think he wanted me out of his team for that.'

'What are you talking about? I want to meet him,' he said.

'Sure, he has called for an announcement party today where the media is guessing that he'll announce his next project.'

The two were struggling to connect the dots as they decided to head straight to Zubin's party at the Sun 'n' Sand Hotel in Juhu.

It was a grand spectacle doing ample justice to the persona of Zubin Mistry. The bigwigs of the film industry, print and television media and socialites were there in large numbers. Soon, Zubin took centre stage and in a sharp departure from his unruly antics, he greeted all his guests rather cordially. He was welcomed amidst a round of applause as one of the producers went ahead and garlanded him.

'Bloody hypocrite,' murmured Emma as Zubin's purported sobriety and grace continued for a few minutes.

Dhruv was still trying to make sense of what was happening. He remembered Zubin telling him that his story, The Most Successful Failure, would be his next project in all probability. However, Dhruv hadn't been contacted. Nevertheless, he somehow kept his restlessness at bay and attended to the proceedings of the event.

Zubin, in a euphoric voice, declared, 'Ladies and gentlemen, my next film goes on floors by the end of the month and I have invited you all today to share with you that in my opinion, my next film will be my most challenging and satisfying experience.'

The resounding claps and celebratory call-outs from the crowd were in sharp contrast to Dhruv's contemplative silence. Zubin then said, 'The film is tentatively titled "The

Most Successful Failure".

The crowd went up in cheers as the oxymoronic title had profound depth. It rang an even louder bell in Dhruv's mind and he looked towards Emma in disbelief. Emma signalled him to hold his horses, as Zubin continued, 'Oh God... Friends, you won't believe who gave me the idea for this one.'

Dhruv was in tears, his hands were cold, his lips trembling and his ears were itching to hear the right name.

'It was none other than my beautiful fiancée, Laura,' he said.

The words struck Dhruv like a thunderbolt. He was dumbfounded for a minute. His parched mouth was gasping for breath. Emma caught the despondent look on his face. She, too, was flustered and broken to hear what Zubin had just uttered.

'You see, we film-makers think that we have a copyright on creativity, but then, as they say, ideas come from the most unexpected of places. And Laura, my love, you have no idea what a gem you came up with that night,' he smiled as his much younger fiancée continued blushing.

The atmosphere was one of camaraderie and fun at the Sun 'n' Sand Hotel, when suddenly an angst-ridden voice came from amongst the crowd. It was Dhruv. He shouted out loud, 'This is my work, my idea and my script.' Dhruv was livid as he charged towards Zubin, only to be stopped by security officials around. Zubin continued feigning ignorance as a wry smile from him needled an already agitated Dhruv.

'Calm down...calm down,' smiled Zubin.

'I narrated this script to you on Floor IX of the studio, you perverted thief. I—and not some Laura, or whoever you wish to marry—came up with this idea, you worthless scumbag!'

Dhruv spat at him from a distance as the situation got ugly and he was forcibly pulled away from the spot. Emma tried to calm his temper, however the situation had turned ugly.

'Be kind with him,' spoke out the supposedly magnanimous and kind-hearted Zubin. 'My heart goes out to young people like him. They work hard, come from a small town with dreams in their eyes and they wish for instant success. And, when that doesn't happen, they go crazy,' he sympathized.

Zubin didn't even break a sweat as he raised a toast to the creative genius of his fiancée Laura. Dhruv was close to being roughed up by the guards, as Emma played peacemaker and calmed them down. As the guards left, a distraught Dhruv sat down crying in the parking lot. Emma too was broken to see him.

'Emma, he stole my script, God dammit! What do I do?' he cried in pain.

'Dhruv, we have to act smartly here,' she cautioned. 'They're powerful people and we can't fight them. We'll have to request and persuade them,' she said.

'Request for what?' Dhruv asked, brimming with rage. 'Request for credit for something that I created?' he asked out of despair, kicking a nearby pillar in the parking lot.

A totally wrecked and enraged Dhruv let out a groan of helplessness as his back slid down the pole he was standing against and he sat down there, placing his head on his knees, howling inconsolably. Emma too was in tears. She knew how much it meant to Dhruv. It was as if a part of Dhruv's soul had been unceremoniously snatched away from him.

'Dhruv…Dhruv…honey, please listen…' Emma tried to talk him out of his despair.

'Son of a bitch, I didn't see this coming!' Dhruv continued fuming and crying alternatively.

Emma affectionately hugged him like a child and caressing his hair, she said, 'Honey, it's important for you to have a calm conversation with Zubin.'

Dhruv was too disillusioned to make sense of the situation.

'Honey…listen…' Emma turned his face towards herself and continued, 'You have to talk it out with him.'

Dhruv gradually calmed down a bit as a sense of purpose began gripping him.

Emma said, 'I'll go and ask him to give you one patient hearing. We have no other option.'

A determined Emma hugged him tightly and then headed backstage, as the event drew to a close. She literally ran up to Zubin, jostling against a dozen others who were surrounding him. Gasping for breath, she finally made it and said, 'Sir, may I have a minute?'

Zubin nonchalantly looked at her and nodded in the affirmative without uttering a word. Emma followed him backstage into his room.

'This is what I get for giving in to the demands of my novice assistants. I heard this guy out only because of you and what do I get in return?' spoke out Zubin.

Emma abhorred every minute of Zubin's hypocrisy and clear obfuscation, however she didn't lose her temper. Collecting herself, she said rather calmly, 'Sir, you're a stalwart, but please try and understand, you and I both know that the boy you met that day wasn't an ordinary talent. He worships his craft and I request you to please do justice to him.' Emma was inching towards breaking down as she requested Zubin with folded hands.

After a minute of silence, Zubin said, 'Fine, send him in.' He drank what was left of his wine. Emma humbly thanked him and went out to call Dhruv.

A visibly tense yet focussed Dhruv entered the room. Deep inside, he was fuming; however, on the outside, he sought reconciliation.

'Come Dhruv, have a seat,' Zubin said, pouring some wine into his glass. Dhruv gingerly sat down on the chair.

Zubin sighed and said, 'Really sorry to hear about your father.' Dhruv accepted his condolences.

'And also sorry for what happened out there. My mistake that I didn't have a word with the original writer of the film,' he said, much to Dhruv's relief.

Dhruv too reciprocated by trying to apologise for the outburst, but Zubin insisted that there wasn't any need for him to do so.

Taking a gentle sip of the wine, he said, 'Dhruv, what is the final message of the story that you've written?'

'Salvation lies within,' replied Dhruv.

'These are profound words indeed, and so very apt for today's situation. That's the genius of your writing, Dhruv. Three simple words sum up the essence of life,' he philosophized with a wry smile. Dhruv wasn't able to fathom as to where the conversation was heading.

'Salvation lies within, Dhruv. You know it better than me. You're the writer of the story—The Most Successful Failure. That's your salvation kid! Why do you need credit for that? You just know it from within,' he said.

A fuming Dhruv tried to reason, 'Because that is the truth, Zubin. The credit should go to the creator. The truth should prevail.'

'Truth...' smiled Zubin, as he continued, 'Of all the lies in the world, the most misleading one is about the existence of truth. There is no absolute truth. It's all illusory and the whole world is an illusion. That's what your story is all about, isn't it?... Anyway, Dhruv, tell me, do you have a copyright of the script that you gave me?' asked Zubin.

'No,' replied Dhruv.

'Hmmm... Any intimation or notification given to you by me or my staff in receipt of your script?'

A hesitant 'no' was Dhruv's answer.

Zubin came a little forward on his chair and bending towards Dhruv, he looked him in the eye and said, 'Now that's truth.'

Dhruv was flustered and frozen at the same time.

'Calm down, kid, calm down. I was just telling you about the hollowness of the word "truth". Frankly, it sucks. But you are in here with a reasonable man, so no need to fear, 'cause I believe in justice. Well, justice and truth sound quite similar but only the wise realize the difference between the two. I know you're wise,' Zubin smiled.

After a moment of silence, he said, 'Twenty grand.'

Dhruv was livid. He had never attached a price tag on his craft.

'Fine, I understand, you're passing through a rough phase, Dhruv. Forty grand, and I think we have a deal,' Zubin said with a hint of optimism.

It was one of those rare moments for Dhruv when one just stands apart and observes the situation as a ringside viewer. Time just stood still for that second as Dhruv thought: *Here I am discussing a deal for a script that was conceptualized by me on a winter morning at four. It was shaped, moulded and stitched together with my blood, sweat and tears for months together. Wonder what the breakdown of these forty grand would be? Maybe it is ten grand for the unrelenting passion, perhaps fifteen to twenty grand for those sleepless nights of despair when not a single idea or thought could be set in motion despite hours of nerve-wracking ruminations. Oh God, perhaps the credit title, 'Written by', is just an understatement for one man's lifetime of dreams and hopes... And this man wants to barter that for forty grand?*

'What are you thinking, Dhruv?' asked Zubin.

Dhruv tuned back in to the moment, snapping out of his chain of thoughts. He came closer to Zubin and in a mild tone, he asked, 'Is there anyone around?'

Zubin smiled and said, 'Don't worry, no one is remotely around at this moment. No one will ever know what happened between us here.' Zubin thought he sensed a breakthrough.

'Oh that's great,' said Dhruv. 'You know, Zubin, "Salvation lies within" is a profound thought indeed. I've written it, but perhaps I haven't graduated to that level yet. For today, my salvation lies in this...'

What came next was a tight, stinging slap across Zubin's face. He was stunned. Before he could even speak, boom came another one. One after the other, Dhruv gave him his version of salvation.

'Sshhh!' Dhruv told him. 'Now you lawyer up, asshole, 'cause I'm coming after you in the court.'

Zubin looked like a frightened little child, as Dhruv left, but not without another parting shot across Zubin's face.

Chapter 9

Love Knows Not Its Depth

*D*hruv had filed a legal complaint against Zubin. He was accompanied by Emma as the two discussed the matter with the counsel.

'Your case is not watertight,' said the attorney. Dhruv knew that very well, but he was in for a fight.

'But it is the truth, and I feel truth shall prevail,' he said.

'We'll fight it to the last,' assured the attorney, as Dhruv wrote him a cheque for his services. Mired in litigation and debts, his tense hand wasn't very smooth while signing the cheque.

'It'll work out, don't worry,' assured the attorney.

Emma and Dhruv had a rather quiet dinner at a roadside restaurant in suburban Mumbai. The two were helping themselves, when a disillusioned Dhruv just abandoned the spoon and sat back on his chair. He seemed totally dispirited and shattered.

After a moment of silence, Emma quietly asked him, 'Was it under the ear or on the cheek?'

Dhruv looked at her with surprise and said, 'It was actually *on* the ear.'

'Hmm… Zubin was always fond of music,' she said.

'Yes, I heard that he likes loud rock music,' said Dhruv.

'Especially the kind with different beats,' she said.

'Oh, he heard four different beats, each more melodious than the other one.'

Emma burst out laughing. Dhruv too laughed his lungs out.

'You bet he'll not forget this beating for a long time!' exclaimed Emma, barely able to speak amidst the bout of laughter. Dhruv continued laughing as he held his stomach and sides. It had been a welcome respite after a month of grief and heartbreak.

The laugh slowly metamorphosed into tears, which began rolling down Dhruv's cheeks. Emma held his hand and with tears in her own eyes, she said, 'This too shall pass.'

Dhruv nodded and hugged her tightly. He kissed her forehead as she warmly cuddled him. It had been an emotionally tumultuous phase for the two. However, the rising waves hadn't yet found their shore and perhaps the brewing storm was readying itself for more carnage.

After a minute of silence, Emma said, 'Dhruv, I'm going back home, day after tomorrow.'

Dhruv was dead silent as a shadow literally passed over his face and he asked, 'And when are you coming back?'

'I don't know, Dhruv. Maybe I won't come back ever. It actually depends on you... Depends on where you see the two of us in the future,' she said.

Dhruv took a deep breath and said, 'I've always seen the two of us together, walking hand in hand along the beach right till the sunset of our lives, but then...'

'But what Dhruv?' she asked.

'But then reality wakes me up and tells me that you deserve better.' Dhruv was struggling for words; his emotions seemed to get the better of him. Emma too was on the brink of a breakdown, as Dhruv somehow mustered up enough courage to continue, 'Emma, I'll never forget that day on Floor IX of the studio. That day, there were a million emotions that I felt, but the one emotion that stood out for me was a promise that I'm going to keep you happy, no matter what. Your happiness is the most precious thing to me in this world.'

He held her hand and said, 'You deserve better than this Emma. You deserve better than a man mired in litigations, debts and broken dreams. I am nothing but a ruined man, Emma.'

Emma, in an assuring tone, said, 'We'll together build a castle from amongst these ruins, Dhruv.'

Emma's words exuded her zest for life, characteristic to her persona.

Touched by her gesture, Dhruv said, 'That's the Emma I know—full of life and positivity.'

Kissing her hand, he said, 'Keep smiling, Emma. I know you never complain about anything. You deserve someone who can share your laughs, multiply your joys and give you all the happiness that you truly deserve. Alas, that someone is perhaps not Dhruv.' His voice started choking but with great effort, he continued, 'Years from now, Emma, you'll look back at this day and thank your stars that you didn't end up with me in this mess of debts and litigations.'

'Thank my stars…' Emma repeated Dhruv's words and asked him, 'Who knows what our stars have in store for us, Dhruv? It's all about making good of what we have today, but you don't get that.'

'Emma, I can't be selfish and ruin your life, knowing fully well that I am in no position to give you a prosperous life. I'm sorry, Emma, but I can't…I just can't,' he broke down in desperation.

'So is it all over, Dhruv?' Emma asked despondently. The reality had started sinking in, as Emma too broke down. The two hugged each other tightly and cried their hearts out. Dhruv kept whispering, 'I'm sorry,' as the two felt devastated.

As they were crying in pain, a little gang of beggars on the roadside sang a melancholic song: 'Love knows not its depth, till the hour of separation.' The beggars were asking the pedestrians and passersby for money in return for their effort. Perhaps they understood precious little about the words of the song.

Emma got up and went to meet a little beggar girl who was singing her heart out. Emma's tears hadn't dried yet as she smiled towards the girl and gently ruffled her hair. The girl was so focused on her craft that she didn't let Emma's affection come in the way of her performance: 'Strange are the ways of the heart. The more they love, the more they hurt.'

Wonder what was more heart-rending—the poetry of her words or the tears rolling down Emma's cheeks. Emma gave her a note, which the girl gleefully accepted. She continued singing with even greater gusto, as Emma kissed her forehead and turned away, carrying with her a scarred memory for life.

Dhruv sat there, numb and powerless. A litany of thoughts was gatecrashing his mind, which was already ravaged by an onslaught of pain and loss.

He wondered whether he should get up and stop Emma. His beating heart tempted his mind, but for Dhruv, Emma's eventual happiness was sacrosanct. Dhruv's restraint was the hallmark of selfless love, as he watched Emma go. *She'll be happy*, was his silent prayer, as it opened up a floodgate of tears and emotional outburst in Dhruv. The only thing worse than a heartbreak is perhaps the insensitivity meted out towards it by the hands of fate.

Barely had his tears dried that Dhruv got a phone call from his uncle who frantically told him about how the creditors had vandalized his home. They had warned Dhruv against leaving Banaras for a long time. Dhruv had tried to reason, but then, reason is the first sacrificial lamb at the altar of creditors and loan sharks. He had to immediately rush back to Banaras. Dhruv hung up and sat back for a minute. It was a battle of survival for Dhruv. He realized that it was time that he dug his heels in and reclaimed his business and property.

'Bloody scoundrels brought this wall down,' muttered his uncle, Vidur, as Dhruv stood amidst the ruins of the boundary walls of his house.

'I tried stopping them, brother, but they just didn't listen,' said his son Rishi, rallying behind Dhruv.

'Son, your father and I grew up together. Yes, we parted ways; perhaps, I couldn't keep pace with him, but nothing can negate our relationship. And just remember, Dhruv, you're not alone in this world.' Vidur fondly remembered Ram and said, 'He was always very proud of you, Dhruv. We seldom spoke in the last few years but whenever we did, he would only talk about you.'

Dhruv pondered for a while, lost in introspection and some soul-searching.

'Hmmm... What are you doing these days, Rishi?' Dhruv asked.

Rishi hesitantly replied, 'Nothing much brother, I'm...I'm nearly a graduate now. Except for Advanced Economics, I have cleared all my papers.' Rishi's career had been like a plane that was always waiting to crash even before it had taken off.

There was a renewed sense of purpose in Dhruv. He thought for a minute and said, 'I am going to rebuild this business—Baba's business.' Every word was steady, balanced and had a steely resolve.

'I am going to pay all the debts and restore this house to its past glory,' he declared.

'We're with you, son,' reaffirmed Vidur.

The next day, he met the creditors and told them that he would not be going anywhere till he paid them every single penny that his father ever took. So mission-oriented was he, that he took all the slander and indignation from the creditors in his stride without getting provoked. He did not retaliate. Both Vidur and Rishi accompanied him everywhere.

Dhruv finally reached his father's office, a shadow of its former self. 'Samrat Stones and Pearls' read the tattered banner. An overflowing waste basket stood near the door. Dhruv opened the lock and entered along with his uncle and cousin, taking a walk around the place. His uncle kept sharing anecdote after anecdote about how Ram and he would travel more than twenty miles every day to set up the business. Dhruv was listening to him carefully, as Vidur continued, 'But your father was very hardworking and I couldn't keep pace with him.' He then smiled apologetically and said, 'I guess that's why one day he relieved me of my duties.' After a moment of awkward silence, Vidur continued, 'But the magnanimous big brother that he was, he set up a similar shop for me across the river and didn't charge me a penny for that. I'll never forget that gesture, Dhruv, but I let myself and him down again. The shop closed down within five years.

I think I didn't ever have it in me,' he said.

Dhruv kept a reassuring hand on his shoulder and said, 'Don't think that way, Uncle. We'll set this up together and we'll do it for Baba.'

Vidur was moved to tears as he said, 'We're with you, my son.' Holding Dhruv's hand in a gesture of gratitude, he said, 'We're in your service, my beloved. Tell the old man how he and his son can help you from here on.'

For the next few days, Dhruv worked long hours in his office. The sword of the ever-escalating debts, courtesy the interest rates, was hanging over his head. Rishi and Vidur were assisting him in the operations.

'Pearls, stones and their mysticism...' Dhruv wondered how much of a study they would entail. There were more than a hundred varieties of stones. Some were worn for general reasons like wealth and health, while others were for specific goals like controlling temper and improving investments. And then there were others that promised mental peace and a steady mind.

Legend had it that Dhruv's forefathers were alchemists and could transform ordinary lead into gold, through severe penance. *What was it? Was is just belief, superstition or was there scientific justification for this?* Dhruv wondered. He remembered how he used to enquire the same of his father, who would always greet his queries with a prophetic smile. Perhaps the answer to this was destined to be sought by Dhruv himself. It was a rare moment of epiphany during this gross introspection that made Dhruv note down the words, 'The Alchemists', on a piece of paper.

'Samrat's Stones and Pearls' was hence renamed as 'The Alchemists'.

It was just the first of many such initiatives that Dhruv took to revamp his family business. He forged tie-ups with exporters in Delhi. During the course of this struggle, Vidur would, time and again, craftily raise the question of their monetary compensation. Dhruv finally decided to address the moot issue.

'Uncle, you know my financial position. You know about the cash coming in and the piled-up debts,' he said.

'Of course, I know that son. And trust me, both Rishi and I do not wish to burden you with our worries anymore than you already are,' he said.

'I can't give you anything right now. All I can offer you both is a partnership in the company,' said Dhruv, realizing that it was perhaps the only offer that could hold them back.

Vidur accepted the offer with both hands. The Alchemists was now a partnership company with equal share between Dhruv and Vidur.

Chapter 10

The Ghat of Redemption

Within a couple of months, the dilapidated, lifeless office began bustling with activity. Dhruv had got on board some people who could help him understand the craft of mining, polishing and preparing different gems and stones. One such day, Dhruv took a long walk down the steps of Manikarnika Ghat. It was here that he used to occasionally sit and reflect on the happenings of his life. It was Dhruv's go-to place for introspection, the place where his parents were cremated.

'You love this place, don't you?' Dhruv heard a familiar voice. It was the old priest who had had a mystical connection with Dhruv from the day he was born; the priest who had named him 'Dhruv'. The two shared a rather informal relationship, the kind that seemed wry and blunt on the outside, but was special deep down. His prophetic smile was intact, and going by his jibes, his razor sharp wit also hadn't lost its sting.

'You're more of a sadist than a priest, I feel,' Dhruv replied.

The priest had a hearty laugh.

'Well if I am a sadist, wonder what you think of the Almighty. He's perhaps the leader of the Sadistic Hall of Fame,' he shot back.

Dhruv wore a nonchalant look. He seemed in no mood to

argue with the priest. The priest descended a couple of steps and sat next to Dhruv.

'I am in a mess, you realize that,' said Dhruv.

'I do, actually. But I also know that you are one tough guy who can rise above this and come back stronger,' said the priest, munching on some peas and nuts.

Offering Dhruv the same, he continued, 'Come on, rise above...that's what you're all about. Hell, I've seen you rise above all the naysayers' prophecies and be born on that fateful day to begin with.'

'You have no sensitivity whatsoever,' Dhruv said.

'Well, I am not good with words you see. That's why I am a priest and not a sage,' he said.

'I've had enough,' Dhruv said and got up to go. He had climbed a couple of steps when he heard the priest calling him, 'Dhruv...'

'What?' he said, turning.

'Come on, you have been a fighter since birth. You beat all the odds and the naysayers' warnings to be born on that fateful day. Nothing could stop you from coming into this crazy universe, not even the worst of riots and storms... There was a reason why you were named Dhruv. Look up at the sky, there are thousands of stars. Many of them break away and explode into oblivion but the one that keeps shining the brightest, unwavering and steady, is Dhruv, the shining star.'

Dhruv registered the priest's words and said, 'Seems you're actually turning into a sage.'

The priest laughed and said, 'I guess that is someone else's destiny, not mine. I am happy being a priest.'

'It's better to live one's own destiny imperfectly rather than being a poor imitation of someone else's perfection.' The quote connected deeply with Dhruv at so many levels that he felt drawn to the Hindu religious epic, the Bhagavad Gita. Thereafter, he spent long hours after work studying the book in great detail. Some sections of the book appealed immensely to him, and then there were some he didn't connect with at all.

'Whatever happened was good, what's happening now is very well, and whatever will happen, will be for the good' was one such quote that he was trying hard to understand.

Working and studying till late in the night, Dhruv's only respite was taking long walks along the Assi Ghat where his companion was mostly some good old traditional turmeric tea. It was while sipping this tea one evening that Dhruv took a walk along a chequered path—the path down memory lane. It was the lane marked with grief and pain, but there were also moments of elation that didn't fail to put a smile across his face.

'Waltz with the princess...' Dhruv remembered his first dance with Emma. The racing hearts, the careless whispers, the touch of divinity—Dhruv was overwhelmed with nostalgia.

The thing about nostalgia is that it is a bittersweet feeling that brings unbridled joy, ushering in cherished memories from the forgotten recesses of your mind but at the same time, it also unlocks cravings and longings that one had clamped down with great effort. The clamps, however, had given way and Dhruv had begun longing for Emma. The longing soon assumed greater proportion as Dhruv impulsively took out his phone and started searching for her number. Mustering some courage, he finally dialled the number.

A familiar voice greeted him from the other side. For Dhruv, it was a moment of joy laced with pain and longing, as he hesitated and said, 'Emma…'

He couldn't speak a word beyond.

Emma, on the other side, too, was going through a plethora of emotions. She somehow braved them all, and in a sporting way, broke the ice and cheerfully said, 'Is that Dhruv Samrat, the famous man of pearls and stones from India?'

Dhruv smiled and nodding in delight, he said, 'Yes ma'am, you must check out our exquisite collection next time you come to Banaras.'

Emma had a good laugh and said, 'Thanks, but I doubt that's ever going to happen again.'

'Somebody once told me, "Never say never!" Who knows what destiny has in store?' Dhruv replied.

'Hmm… That somebody must be a genius, I tell you,' she laughed.

'I agree,' he said with a cheerful smile. And then followed a moment of silence. It wasn't an awkward silence, which is generally symptomatic of a severed relationship, but a silence of bliss where perhaps each had, by now, found their redemption. Dhruv and Emma were comfortable even in each other's silences.

'Emma, thanks a lot,' said Dhruv.

'For what?' she asked.

'For taking my call even when you're totally justified in not speaking to me ever again,' he said.

'What's happened is behind us, Dhruv. Let's move ahead,' she said, putting up a brave front even though the pain of parting ways was apparent in both their voices.

'Dhruv, what time is it in India?' she asked.

'It's one o'clock. God, it's late in here,' said Dhruv.

'Hmm… And if I am guessing correctly, this time around

The Ghat of Redemption

you must be at Assi Ghat sipping some turmeric tea,' she said.

Dhruv was rather touched to know how well she knew him. The two discussed their lives back and forth. Engrossed in a dialogue over the phone, Dhruv seemed to be in a paradise of his own.

Rishi had been looking for his cousin for a long time. He finally found Dhruv perched on one of the steps of the ghat, gazing at the Ganges in front. Rishi sat next to him and seeing Dhruv engrossed in a myriad of thoughts, Rishi softly said, 'You still love her like crazy, don't you?'

Dhruv didn't say a word. His longing eyes told quite a story, though.

'Brother, you should not have let her go,' said Rishi.

Dhruv looked towards Rishi and in a voice ridden with purpose, he said, 'I have not given up on us yet.'

A surprised Rishi waited to hear more, as Dhruv continued, 'But I didn't hold her back. You look at the holy Ganges, Rishi, pure and sacred. The Ganges asks for nothing from us, except perhaps a bit of love. From the snow-clad Himalayas to the ethereal land of Banaras and right up till the Bay of Bengal, it flows majestically uninhibited, unhindered.' Dhruv sighed and continued, 'Nobody holds it back. Emma, too, like the Ganges, is precious and sacred. She should never be held back because of one man's turmoil. She is meant to flow and express freely in life. But, yes, if ever there comes a day when I am able to wriggle out of my deep mess, I'll walk up to her and this time, I'll never let her go...'

He sighed and repeated, 'Never ever let her go,' with emotions seeping out of every pore of his body.

Chapter 11

Emma's World

Emma Schellenberg had grown up in an orphanage in suburban Geneva. She was told that her parents had abandoned her and that her arrival into the universe was unwanted and untimely. The scars of that truth were often camouflaged by Emma's vibrant smile, which exuded warmth and optimism. She was different. For her, life was always about smelling the roses, counting your blessings and celebrating the imperfections. Perhaps all she sought was some unconditional love, which had eluded her since childhood. And then came Dhruv, a victim of circumstances himself, who loved her selflessly. Alas! The circumstances had gotten the better of his selfless love.

Emma had hung up on a cheerful note and wished Dhruv lots of success for his venture. Now, leaning back on her rocking chair, within the confines of her rather modest yet vibrant studio apartment, she looked up towards the Almighty with a smile and a silent prayer on her lips.

She then browsed through her handbag and took out a business card that belonged to one Jamie Maxwell. Emma gave the card a long stare. Lost in a myriad of thoughts, she woke up to the moment, when her doorbell rang. She opened the door and saw a bright young man from the State Department waiting for her.

'Hi Nick,' she greeted him.

'Ms Emma Schellenberg, we confirm as per reports and records that Mr Jamie Maxwell from downtown south is your biological father,' said Nick.

Emma couldn't believe her ears. Even though Emma was abandoned at birth, she had been on a quest to find out about her biological parents. It had taken her to state departments and hospital authorities. From pillar to post she tried connecting the links, until she finally found out that Jamie Maxwell was her father. A bankrupt alcoholic, Maxwell had been living off the security programme of the Swiss Government.

Emma's heart was pounding with nervous excitement and a sense of anticipation as her car reached her destination. As she stepped out, there was an avalanche of thoughts and emotions in her mind. Devoid of parental love and blessings, Emma had longed for this day. However, the fact that she was abandoned by them made her sad to the point where she felt totally broken from inside. It was the moment of truth for her, and after all considerations, she graciously smiled and decided to bite the bullet as she knocked on the door.

A seemingly washed out, unkempt old man opened the door. He seemed listless and drunk. Scratching his dishevelled grey beard, he said, 'What can I do for you?'

Emma was breathing heavily as the security officer asked the old man his name.

'Jamie Maxwell,' he said out loud.

The words reverberated in Emma's ears and tugged at her heartstrings as the realization dawned on her—she was seeing her father right before her eyes! For a second, she was totally numb and got cold feet. Meanwhile, an old woman too came out. She was surprised to see the officer and a young lady. She asked her husband, who also seemed clueless. The two exchanged a few barbs and started quarrelling. Emma kept looking at the woman's eyes; they were large, expressive and green. Emma smiled and closed her eyes, as a tear ran down her cheek.

The officer then took the couple to a corner and told them about their biological relationship with the lady standing there. Mr and Mrs Maxwell were dumbstruck at what they were hearing and seeing.

A young green-eyed beautiful lady stood before them. 'Look at her bracelet,' she murmured to her husband.

'Is it gold?' he asked.

The wife nodded and feigning an affectionate smile, she went up to Emma and patted her cheeks.

'You're a beautiful girl,' she said.

Emma smiled back and held her hand as the two sat down. The old woman was quick to observe that Emma also wore a gold pendant. Emma was so consumed in the moment that she could barely gauge the lust and greed in Mrs Maxwell's eyes.

'When you were born, I told Jamie that she'll grow up to be a beautiful woman one day, and look at you,' she said with a sly smile.

'Why did you leave me then?' asked Emma with tears barely clinging on to her eyelashes, ready to give in to gravity any second.

Mrs Maxwell started crying out loud in an exaggerated display of melodrama. Her husband meanwhile was still puzzled at what was unfolding before his eyes. All he knew was that Emma could be his potential cash cow and foot his alcohol bills.

Mrs Maxwell then said, 'We were not ready for you. Your father was a useless man—he still is useless—and we couldn't afford you.'

'It was a mistake,' said Jamie, feigning regret.

'What? Conceiving me or abandoning me?' asked an emotionally charged Emma, as tears began rolling down from her eyes.

The two very strategically rallied around her and apologized for their actions. Emma politely asked them to keep a distance and regaining her composure, she said, 'You never thought about me all this while.'

'We did sweetheart, but your father was broke all through. This useless piece of crap...' she said, looking at him.

Emma was vulnerable and despite all her grouses against them, she felt a certain kind of elation at seeing her parents.

'Strange are the ways of the Lord,' said Mrs Maxwell. 'Emma, we know, we've been horrible, but won't you forgive your parents?' She crookedly struck all the right chords.

Emma wiped her tears and with her characteristic forgiving smile, she said, 'I don't hold anything against you anymore. Just that it hurt sometimes.'

Mrs Maxwell hugged her rather dramatically and in an overt display of pseudo-affection, she said, 'Our daughter has come home... Just a while back I was telling your father how I wish we had a child who could take care of us...'

Emma returned to her apartment both overwhelmed and emotionally drained.

'Phew...' she exhaled a couple of times and before she

could repeat for the third time, she just broke down. In the confines of the four walls, emotions that had been bottled up for quite a while burst forth and she wept piteously that night.

Sometimes, I just imagine that you're sitting next to me, with an impish smile adorning your face, lit up beautifully by those prism-like green eyes, through which I wish to view the universe. Who says that time doesn't wait? It waits every time you smile and nod, every time you move your lips to say my name... I miss you... I miss the warmth of your touch, the serenity of your presence and the calming assurance of your words...

A tear fell on the paper, smudging some ink as Dhruv looked up and closed his eyes for a while. His pen had been his medium of catharsis during his longing for Emma. However, his resolve to go back to her one day was perhaps even more intense than his longing.

The Alchemists, Dhruv's rechristened business, had grown satisfactorily over the last few months. His tireless efforts had started bearing fruit. Dhruv, the artist, often wondered how Dhruv, the entrepreneur, would cope with the cold and calculative world of deals and negotiations. Little did he know that his creative side possessed a disarming charm that would ensure that he didn't need to employ any shrewd tactics for the advancement of his business. He had masterfully blended the mystique surrounding pearls and stones with the narrative of his business.

During the course of this struggle, Dhruv had embarked on many journeys. One was of material advancements, which would help him pay off his debts, restore his father's honour and go back to Emma. The other journey was a rather silent yet deep one. It was a journey within his mind, a journey that was abstract and yet so real—a spiritual journey.

He would at times sit with the priest at the ghats and discuss what he had read about different pearls, stones and their properties.

'I can't believe how closely linked planets, stars, chakras and pearls are,' exclaimed Dhruv.

The priest smiled and chanted, '*Hari om.*'

'No, seriously,' Dhruv continued. 'I never believed in all this, and generally dismissed it as far-fetched mythology, but I think that there is more to this universe than we know,' he thought out loud. 'A ruby, a sapphire or an opal stone—they are all there for a specific purpose. It's unbelievable how big a role stars and planets play in our lives.'

'Tell me one thing—is it all destined or do we make it happen with our actions?' he curiously asked.

'Maybe it's written,' said the priest with a sense of mystery.

'Or maybe I'm writing it,' Dhruv contemplated aloud.

The priest smiled and gave Dhruv some food for thought. He said, 'Ask yourself this question. Do you think whatever has happened with you thus far is pre-written?'

Dhruv pondered for a while and said, 'Maybe it was written. Otherwise why would I end up trading pearls and stones rather than being a storyteller or a film-maker?'

The priest smiled and said, 'How do you know this is the end? Maybe it's just the beginning.'

Dhruv thought for a while and said, 'It's too complicated.'

He was a creative individual with a scientific bent of mind. Mythology, cosmic energy and spirituality always fascinated him, but the pragmatist in him had always doubted them. However, a deeper dive into these subjects had got him questioning, and seeking some answers.

Meanwhile, Vidur and Rishi had, by now, tasted blood, and had started siphoning off business money for their personal use. They were as sugar-coated as they were sly and Dhruv was too consumed in his work to notice. Dhruv was also attending hearings for the case he had filed against film-maker Zubin Mistry for allegedly plagiarizing his story. The hearings were a painful experience for Dhruv. Striving to prove your claim on something that you so assiduously created, is an inexplicable agony. Mistry's attorney had left no stone unturned in deriding and undermining Dhruv with scathing condescension. Dhruv's troupe members, who had travelled to Mumbai to perform a skit based on his story, had testified in Dhruv's favour, but there was still no concrete proof that Dhruv could present to substantiate his charges. Emma's testification against Zubin could seal things in Dhruv's favour. However, he was absolutely clear about not troubling her and dragging her to court for the hearings.

Emma, on the other side, was in a state of gullibility, where she was trying to make peace between a lonely past and an illusionary present. She was drawn to her parents even though she was aware that they had abandoned her as an infant.

But, they are still my parents, she thought to herself at the end of every bout of brooding over this new development in her life. Emma did finally visit her parents again. They welcomed her with open arms and wide eyes, feverishly browsing for any gold or fortune that they could somehow get their lustful grip on.

Emma's mother, Marla, affectionately cuddled her and kissed her forehead. 'I knew my daughter would not be as bad as we've been. She'll not leave us at the mercy of government security and food stamps,' she said shrewdly.

A gullible Emma gave into Marla's extravagant display of affection. She met the officers of the state department and offered to take custody of her parents. Her alcoholic father had a couple of cases and fines slammed against him for drunken driving and assault. Emma cleared the dues and took her parents to her modest apartment.

Emma's parents were worse than scavengers. Their eyes lit up every time they saw food, money or shelter. They were so brazenly greedy, and yet, Emma decided to ignore all of it. She was just trying to live in this make-believe world of hers where she wasn't alone and had a family of her own. As her parents settled down and started gorging on the food, Emma looked towards them with a temporary sense of calm. She then called up Dhruv who was happy and, at the same time, worried for her.

'Emma, it takes a very big heart to accept such people as parents,' said Dhruv over the phone, commending her magnanimity.

'I guess, not forgiving, not letting go of things doesn't help anybody,' she replied. 'You know, Dhruv, I sometimes feel life is too short to hold grudges and bad blood against anyone,' she said, feeling calm after a long spell of anxiety.

Dhruv became a bit emotional on hearing this. How he wished he could cross the seas and tell Emma how much he loved her.

'Emma...'

'Yes?' she said.

'I am really proud of you,' he said.

'For what?' she asked.

'For always being the bigger person without letting the other one think he is small,' he replied.

Today I witnessed purity in its most pious avatar. That avatar is called Emma. You know, it's often seen that many people are beautiful on the outside, but not so from the inside, and vice-versa. Emma is an exception. Her external beauty only gives a glimpse of the celestial beauty that she possesses within.

Dhruv was penning down his thoughts. This habit had become a routine of late. He hoped to read out his thoughts to Emma one day and ask for her hand. Alas! That day still seemed distant. However, Dhruv's undying efforts were closing that distance with every passing day.

Some time later, he was browsing through the account books of his company. The sales had been going from strength to strength. Rishi and Vidur had been tasked with procuring some stones and gems from vendors in Delhi. A closer analysis of the books brought forward a glaring irregularity that caught Dhruv's attention. He immediately called for Rishi and his uncle. As soon as he confronted Rishi with the irregularity, Rishi began to fumble. He was caught red-handed, siphoning money off the company. Dhruv was livid. Vidur had by now sensed that the situation was going out of hand. He slyly got up from his chair and slapped his son across his face.

'You're a disgrace,' he shouted at him furiously.

Rishi was taken by surprise and so was Dhruv, who tried

to calm his uncle down.

'Apologize to your brother, now. I feel ashamed to call you my son,' he fumed with manufactured rage.

'It's okay, Rishi, it's ok...' repeated Dhruv, trying to calm his uncle down, who had very cleverly managed to put a lid on Pandora's box. Rishi, however, silently vowed to never forgive Dhruv for the humiliation he faced that day.

Dhruv dismissed this irregularity as an aberration and shifted his focus to a large deal that he had been working on for some time. He was close to inking a contract with a Delhi-based exporter for some rare pearls. Dhruv started working even longer hours. He had promised the exporter that he would source for him some of the rarest pearls in India. For this, Dhruv did extensive research and travelled to the interiors of the country. Amidst the long rigours of travel and business, there were times when he had to trust Rishi and Vidur.

Dhruv was also closing in on the intellectual property case against Zubin in Mumbai. The case took an interesting turn when Dhruv narrated verbatim some scenes and dialogues from the script. Dhruv claimed that only the creator could know his scenes to this level of precision. This strong argument began tilting scales in favour of Dhruv. However, a tangible proof or witness remained elusive. Emma's statement had now become crucial for the case. She, however, was grappling with issues of her own, thousands of miles away in Switzerland. She had found a support in Nick, her old friend, who had helped her unearth the whereabouts of her parents. Nick too had separated from his wife after a gruelling divorce procedure.

His latest muse was Emma. He would often express his affection towards her but she would politely turn it down. Her heartbeats had Dhruv etched on them deeply and, moreover, she didn't want to be in a relationship at that point of time. However, Nick was quite charming and he was too smitten by Emma to give up on her.

One day, the two were sitting in a vintage Swiss bar, when Nick asked, sipping some soda, 'So Emma, what are your plans?'

'I am not too sure, Nick. I've completed my thesis, my project film, and now probably I'll take up something in an embassy,' she said, weighing her options after her graduation in international relations.

'And what about your newly found parents?' he asked.

Emma thought for a second and said, 'Well, they're my responsibility now and I've decided not to judge them anymore.'

'I understand that, Emma.' He warmly kept his hand on top of Emma's and continued, 'Look Emma, I've known you since graduation and I have no doubts that you have a promising career ahead of you but the only thing bothering me is that you're holding yourself back in life. Just don't do that and everything will be fine.'

Emma smiled, as Nick continued, 'I'm looking for a role in the Swiss Embassy in India. You can also apply and given your experience and internship, you have a good chance of getting a worthy role.'

Emma held his hand and said, 'Nick, I have to thank you today for being there when no one was around. Thank you for caring about my work, my emotions and my future. It means a lot to me. I'm glad that I matter to someone at least.'

Nick came a little closer to her and said, 'For that someone, you mean the world. He is right here before your eyes, Emma. Open your eyes and embrace him in your life and he will never ever leave you.'

Emma hugged him as an organic reaction to the flow of emotions. Nick was elated, and in that moment, he said, 'Let's get married!'

Emma was overwhelmed. She was also circumspect, sceptical and unsure.

'Nick, isn't this too soon?' she asked.

'That's how life is, Emma. You've got to take the leap.' He held her hand and asked, 'Do you trust me, Emma?'

Emma nodded, a bit hesitantly though.

'Then, what's there to worry?' he asked. 'Emma Schellenberg, will you marry me?' said Nick, as his excitement went through the roof.

Emma looked at Nick, lost in a myriad of thoughts. Her dilemma and puzzled look made Nick's exuberance wane a bit. Emma held his hand and said, 'Nick, don't get me wrong, but please give me some time. I really like you, but I don't know if I am ready.'

A shadow passed over Nick's face. 'I'll wait for you Emma,' he said with a sporting smile, which hid his disappointment.

Emma gave him a hug and as she was about to leave, he said, 'Emma, is it because you still haven't got over Dhruv?'

Emma was a bit disturbed on hearing that.

Nick said, 'I know, I've touched a raw nerve here, Emma, but you have to move on in life. Look at him, he has moved on. Hell, I am sure he doesn't even think about you anymore!'

The words pierced through Emma's heart as she left with a chain of interwoven thoughts that weighed her down. As she walked out, she took out her phone and called up Dhruv, who, for some reason, could not take her call. Nick's words continued ringing in her ears for a long time. *I am a forgotten chapter in Dhruv's life*, she thought.

Little did she know that across the seas, along the holy Ganges, there lived a man whose heartbeats had her name etched on them. And he was tirelessly working with a hope that one day he would go back to her forever and ever.

Nick, however, didn't give up. He continued being the good friend that Emma needed, and the two applied for positions in the Swiss Embassy in India.

Chapter 12

The Canvas of Life

Vidur and Rishi welcomed the client with open arms. Dhruv was out of town for a business meeting. Rishi placed the consignment before the client who happily agreed to write a cheque.

'The Alchemists…isn't that your company's name?' he asked before writing the bearer's name. Before Rishi could nod and say 'Yes,' Vidur promptly said, 'No, Sir.'

Rishi was visibly surprised, as he looked towards his father. In a calm and composed voice, Vidur said, 'The name of the company is "Vidur & Sons Pvt Ltd".'

This sent a chill down Rishi's spine as he was too dumbfounded to speak. Vidur collected the cheque and thanked the client. As the client left, Rishi turned around towards his father who wore a wry smile and said, 'You're wondering about what happened here?'

Vidur then placed before him a company registration paper. He had very quietly and stealthily opened up a company of his own titled 'Vidur & Sons Pvt Ltd'. Every single retail order that came to the office was deftly diverted towards his company.

'We will suck out every last drop that is there in The Alchemists,' declared Vidur. Having felt vengeful since the day Dhruv had confronted him, Rishi was overjoyed about

Dhruv's impending destruction.

Dhruv had no clue about the colossal siphoning that his uncle and cousin had undertaken. He was travelling across north India, meeting merchants and artisans, and trying to procure the choicest gems and stones for a deal that could change his fortune. On a train to Lucknow, he took out his diary and started penning down his thoughts for Emma,

> *Today, I paid off almost all of my father's debts. Phew... can't tell you how relieved I am. Emma, I wonder what the look on your face would be when I present you this diary. I bet you'll be smiling with tears in your eyes. You'd be struggling to read it and with a lump in your throat you'll say, 'I love you Dhruv'... and the tears rolling down your cheeks would be the exclamation mark. That day is not very far, Emma. I just hope I get this order.*

Dhruv closed his eyes for a while and a cool breeze from outside gently kissed his face as he took a short nap. He was dreaming about his written words coming to fruition. Due to the theatrical leanings, his imagination was dramatic. A smile spread across his face as he continued to bask in the glory of his dreamland.

It had been a long day for him as his train reached Lucknow in the early hours of the morning. Just then, he got a call. It was his client, quite a heavyweight in the field. Dhruv's heart was pounding as he discussed the intricacies of the coveted order. After a brief five-minute interaction, the client said, 'Dhruv, you've worked really hard on this. Your partners, Mr Vidur and Rishi, are also here.'

Dhruv was surprised to hear that.

Perhaps they were being proactive and diligent, he thought, giving them the benefit of the doubt.

The client continued, 'Dhruv, they have given me your account and payment details. I have to tell you that we are placing the order with you.'

Dhruv's ears had been itching to hear those golden words. It had been a long time since he had heard any good news. A sense of elation filled his heart, as the news began to dawn on him. He humbly thanked his client and promised him the timely delivery of the material. Sighing in relief, he sat down on the bench at the railway platform. It was a moment of catharsis and reflection for him. He sighed repeatedly with a sense of euphoria. Tears of joy began rolling down his cheeks as he covered his face and closed his eyes to let it all sink in. Just then, Dhruv's phone rang. It was Emma. Dhruv answered, and before he could share his good news, Emma very jubilantly said, 'Dhruv, I just got an offer to work for the Swiss Embassy in India.'

Dhruv's joy knew no bounds. Emma coming to India was something Dhruv had dreamt of. It was now going to become a reality.

'Emma...just come over... I can't wait for you,' he said happily.

Dhruv's racing heart rekindled his emotions towards her as he broke down over the phone. Emma couldn't quite gather why he was getting so emotional.

'Emma, I am coming to see you once you arrive,' he said, his voice laced with a sense of purpose.

As Dhruv hung up, he felt as if destiny had finally decided to be kind to him.

'Rishi, have you deposited the cheque?' asked Dhruv over the phone.

Concealing his guilt, Rishi said, 'Yes brother, I have.'

A surprised Dhruv said, 'Okay Rishi, the bank is taking a little longer to clear the cheque than usual. My accounts don't show the credited amount. I wonder how I'll purchase the goods.'

Rishi hurriedly said, 'Brother, sometimes it takes a little extra time. There is nothing to worry about.'

Dhruv accepted that and said, 'Fine, I'll dig into our savings and buy the goods from Lucknow and then head towards Delhi to hand over the consignment. Meanwhile, just check up with the bank and let me know when the cheque gets cleared.'

Vidur, by now, had already encashed the cheque in favour of his company. Dhruv went ahead with his savings and purchased the remaining stock that had to be delivered to Delhi. Rishi and his father knew that it was now a matter of time before their foul play would come to light, so they were ripping off The Alchemists every way they could.

The canvas of Dhruv's life had never been so multihued. There was a saffron-like dash of hope and resilience, a green splash of deceit gradually thickening, and a yellowish glow of rekindled emotion splattered across the canvas of colours glowing majestically. With hopes and dreams in his heart, Dhruv reached Delhi.

Hope is a strange thing, Emma. It keeps you going and at the same time it instils fear—a fear of the untoward. I

don't know how I am going to be when I meet you. I've played different versions of this scene so many times in my mind. I hope, I don't get nervous or too exuberant when I see you. I hope I am able to articulate to you how much I love you and have always loved you. I hope I can hold your hand and see the same love in your eyes... I hope...

Dhruv had reached the Swiss Embassy in Delhi. It was a huge area with posh lawns and balconies. A cultural programme was underway and hundreds were in attendance. There was an avalanche of emotions in his heart, as his eyes browsed for Emma.

Emma too was looking for him. And then she heard her name.

'Emma!'

It was a familiar voice. Dhruv was shouting out her name from a distance. Emma's gaze found its target and then they exchanged smiles. The drama of the moment was however truly accentuated when the performers dispersed after the thunderous applause. Dhruv and Emma lost sight of each other amidst the ensuing melee. It was almost reminiscent of their first meeting. Perhaps it was ironic that they were always separated by circumstances.

Emma was being congratulated for organizing the event. She was generously accepting the compliments, but her eyes were looking for Dhruv. After a moment or two, Emma zipped past her well-wishers and friends. A pulsating anxiety had gripped her. Dhruv too was breathing heavily and looking around when he suddenly felt a gentle tap on his shoulder. It was Emma.

The two stood there as a moment etched in time. They

didn't speak a word. Perhaps they didn't need to. Then they silently hugged each other. It was warm, affectionate and truly cathartic. The two had weathered so many storms in their lives and despite all the wear and tear, they stood there sharing a moment of affection.

'Woah… It's great to see you,' said Emma, with a heartfelt smile as she gently hugged him again.

Dhruv was so relieved to see her that he just seemed to revel in silence for a brief while. He gently leaned his head against her's and smiled. After a moment he said, 'I've missed you, I've missed you…real bad.'

Emma smiled and said, 'You've lost a few pounds.'

'And you've gained some,' came his reply.

A furious Emma lovingly slapped him on the back, 'You're rude.'

Dhruv laughed and said, 'Hey, but you're looking like a million bucks.'

'Thanks,' she smiled as the conversation between the two flowed almost organically.

Dhruv was waiting for the right moment to bare his heart. Articulating the fact that he still loved her and wanted her back in his life was tough even for a wordsmith like him. *It could sound abrupt. It could even irk her. But dammit the truth is, I love her,* Dhruv thought. Mustering his courage, Dhruv was about to speak when Emma said, 'Dhruv I am really happy to hear about your success. I know what it means to you.'

Dhruv nodded in affirmation, as Emma continued, 'I remember the last time when we met…' She paused for a while as scenes of their painful separation in Mumbai flashed across her mind.

'Oh God…you really needed this,' she smiled.

Dhruv placed his hand on top of her's and said, 'I remember that day, Emma. It was heartbreaking for us but today it has all changed.'

Dhruv was slowly inching towards asking for her hand.

Emma replied, 'It has changed, Dhruv. It has... Look at you today, you're settling down. And guess what? So am I.'

A perplexed Dhruv was all ears, as Emma continued, 'Where do I start? Okay, after I left Mumbai, I was really low and despondent, and it was during this timely hour that I met Nick.'

Dhruv's heart sank deeper with every word, as Emma continued, 'Nick is a great person. Slightly eccentric but still a very loving person. He helps me...'

Emma's words were like repeated thunderbolts on Dhruv's sinking heart.

'And I said yes to him,' said Emma. 'We are getting married, Dhruv,' she jubilantly shared.

Dhruv was a mesh of shattered dreams and dashed hopes. His ears couldn't believe what he had just heard and his eyes almost impulsively began shedding tears.

'What happened?' Emma asked.

Dhruv smiled and said, 'Nothing, I am just happy for you and also for myself.'

Emma hugged him tightly and said, 'Dhruv, you have no idea how difficult it was for me to say yes to Nick. Truth is, Dhruv, I just couldn't get you out of my mind. I had loved you so much that no one could really take that space. But thank God, I finally could allow and picture Nick in that place.'

It was unbearable agony for Dhruv. The tears continued rolling down his cheeks, as the smile across his face tried camouflaging his inexplicable suffering. Perhaps he was smiling at the brutal irony of his love story.

'Nick and I are both serving as assistants to the ambassador in the Swiss Embassy here,' she excitedly shared.

Dhruv receptively nodded, as Emma continued, 'And here is the big news, Nick and I are getting married this Valentine's Day... we have planned a great Indian-style wedding.'

Dhruv was so shell-shocked to hear this that he didn't react at all for a moment. He was in the throes of immense grief and depression. It was so intense that it left him numb. He just wanted to get out of that place. With a straight face, he congratulated Emma and fearing an impending breakdown, he hurriedly said, 'You take care, Emma. I'll see you. I have some work, so we'll catch up later.' He was barely able to form any more words and look her in the eye. Emma found his behaviour a little weird.

'Dhruv, are you okay?' she asked.

'Yes... Yes...absolutely. You take care.'

Dhruv hugged Emma and immediately started walking back.

'Dhruv, is everything alright?' she confirmed again.

Dhruv had, by now, completely broken down. Luckily, his back was turned towards Emma. He somehow mustered enough strength to say, 'Yes', as he walked out. It was a long walk back for Dhruv—a walk he'd remember for a long time.

I took too much time to get back to her, he thought in a fit of desperation. *I should have never let her go,* was another realization that was haunting him to the core.

With every passing second and every step that he took, Dhruv felt as if his whole universe was slipping away right before his eyes. After walking a significant distance down the aisle, he turned back to catch one more glimpse of Emma

The Canvas of Life

who was surrounded with people. He saw her being warmly cuddled by a man. It was Nick. All Dhruv had in his heart and on his lips was a silent prayer for Emma's well-being. He wished her all the happiness in the world. Perhaps this purity was the hallmark of the bond Dhruv and Emma shared. Irrespective of their emotional trajectory, their hearts always wished well for the other.

It was the 14th of February. Emma's D-Day had arrived. The early morning rays of the sun were welcomed by the bride-to-be, as she sat in the lawns of a country club, mulling over the sanctity of the day. There was a palpable uneasiness; an unexplainable anxiety was gripping her. Perhaps it was natural, but then something, somewhere, didn't feel right. Lost in her thoughts, she suddenly felt a tight grasp on her shoulders. It was Nick.

'You scared me,' she shot back. 'Ouch…it's hurting, Nick.'

Nick surprisingly tightened his grasp again.

'Ouch!' she cried out. Nick relaxed his grip and smiled.

'Nick, you were hurting me,' she complained.

'Come on now, sweetheart, that was just a gentle touch,' he smiled, placing his arms around her shoulders.

'Yeah…right,' she said dismissively.

Nick kissed her hair and said, 'I can't wait for tonight. We are finally getting married. I am really excited…aren't you?'

Emma didn't reciprocate the exuberance but smiled and nodded in agreement.

'Oh come on… I am excited even though it's my third marriage. And you are so low on excitement… I don't get it,' he said rather offhandedly.

'Nick, maybe because it's my first time that it hasn't sunk in yet,' she said.

Nick looked at her blankly as she spoke. He then asked, 'Is Dhruv coming?'

'I don't know,' she replied. 'He is in town. Let's see.'

'Why do you think he'll not come?' asked Nick.

'Well, how would I know his reasons?' she replied.

Nick laughed and said, 'If not you, who would know his reasons?'

Emma frowned and wore a puzzled look.

'No, seriously, why would Dhruv not come when he is in town? Either you don't matter to him that much now or maybe you still matter way too much… Food for thought,' he said.

Emma mulled over his words and wondered what Dhruv might be going through at that moment.

Dhruv, on the other hand, had been extremely anxious due to a plethora of reasons. The pain of losing Emma to someone else had already been gruelling. Besides that, he was also struggling to pay the craftsmen and artisans for their work on the coveted order on which he had been working. The advance payment against the order hadn't yet been credited into his account. Worst was that Vidur and Rishi had not been taking his calls since the last three days. Dhruv wasn't getting a great feeling. Something, somewhere, wasn't feeling right. He called up his office assistant and asked about his uncle and Rishi. The assistant told him that they hadn't been coming for the last three days. Dhruv was extremely perturbed to hear that. He had a final meeting with the client the next day. He decided to hand over the consignment, take up the payment issue and clear his bills.

He was lost in a maze of thoughts when he received a

voice message from Emma: 'Hi, Dhruv... I don't know why, but I am getting very nervous and jittery today. Perhaps that's how it is on the wedding day. Listen... umm... I know with our history and all, it's tough for you, but then Dhruv, you are the only one I can probably call family. My so-called parents are in Switzerland. Yes, I have some friends here, but you are family and you'll always be that. So, I hope it's not a very big ask, but, hey, I need you by my side tonight. Once I'm all ready in my Indian wedding finery, I'll keep an eye out for you and I know, you'll be there for me.'

It was a tough time for Dhruv. He poured some water in a glass and drank it. He played the audio many times over. As much as it pained him, he loved to hear about his place in Emma's life. However, the very next moment it dawned on him that this mattered little, as Emma was about to walk down the aisle with someone else. He realized how unbearable an agony it would be for him to see Emma in the bridal avatar getting married to Nick. How he wished he hadn't let go of his relationship with her back in Mumbai last year. But then he remembered how at that time, he was grappling with his Baba's death, escalating debts, script theft and broken dreams. He forgave himself for a second and then held himself guilty the very next moment. Battling these dilemmas, he sat down and took a deep breath.

The mood at the country club was lively and vibrant. Everybody had a spring in their steps. An Indian wedding for a Swiss couple was a wonderful idea. The music, revelry and great Indian song and dance was in full swing. Given Emma's penchant for Indian culture and traditions, the wedding was perhaps even more 'Indian' in ethos than a conventional Indian marriage.

Emma, who was wearing a red and gold brocade lehenga, delicately put on a maang teeka. The green-eyed beauty had a radiant glow on her face, second only to the star-studded sky on a full-moon night. The bangles, the pendant and the earrings were majestic. However, the ornament that outshone them all was her disarming smile. And that smile blossomed fully a moment later when she saw Dhruv enter her room.

Dhruv was overwhelmed to see Emma in the bridal avatar. His heart showered a thousand blessings on her. Yes he was hurt, but then his love for Emma far outweighed the hurt.

Emma hugged him and said, 'Thanks for coming Dhruv... Thanks... I just don't know why I have been feeling so anxious today.'

Dhruv smiled and said, 'By the way, is there a directly proportional relationship between anxiety and beauty, by any chance?'

'I don't know,' she said, still trying to understand his question.

'Well...seems like there is, 'cause Emma Schellenberg, you've never looked more beautiful,' he smiled, tapping her lovingly on her nose.

Emma blushed a little and said, 'You're a wordsmith-wonder! What are you doing with gems and stones?'

'Well, they have taught me a lot,' he said.

'Gems and stones?' she asked.

'Yes, they taught me something about destiny... Nobody can fight destiny, Emma,' he philosophized.

'That's why I always say, "It's all about smelling the roses",

The Canvas of Life

she winked.

'Now can we focus on your marriage? Or we will just keep on chatting for hours together?' he said.

As Emma did some touch-up, Dhruv mischievously said, 'By the way, Emma, you remember you had told me that you'd beat me in a race anytime, anywhere, even though we know that you always cheat?'

'Anytime, anywhere—and listen, I don't need to cheat to defeat you! You are a featherweight.'

'Oh, really? How about right now to the main gate?'

'Oh wow, Mr Dhruv Samrat! First of all, I am all dressed up and heavy. And secondly, do you really want to be seen as the guy who is running away with the bride?'

Dhruv laughed out loud, 'That will be some sight.'

Emma, in a rapturous burst of laughter said, 'Add to that our history and there you go—a recipe for disaster.'

The two laughed their hearts out. The ripples of laughter didn't stop for a while. It had been ages since the two had enjoyed an unabashed moment of fun and laughter. The evening passed on a similar note. There was dance, music and revelry. Emma braved those anxious bouts and happily tied the knot with Nick. After a fun-filled celebratory evening, Dhruv and Emma bid tearful goodbyes. Emma and Nick were off for a holiday across Europe and their hometown in Switzerland. For Dhruv, it was back to being a lone ranger ready to take on the world and its challenges.

Chapter 13

The Miscarriage of Trust

*D*hruv had the most important meeting of his life scheduled for the day. He carefully collected the packets of gems and stones, as he headed to his client's office in south Delhi. During his journey, he tried calling up Vidur and Rishi, but to no avail. As Dhruv reached the office, he was ushered into the cabin of Harish Manchandani, the chairman of the company. The two met cordially. Manchandani was a leading exporter in the industry.

'Mr Dhruv Samrat, I am so glad you came. I have to rush south to meet my export partner and I was just waiting for your arrival and the material.'

The client, along with his team, checked the material in its entirety. Elated with the quality, he said, 'You've done a great job.'

Dhruv thanked him wholeheartedly. The consignment was collected by Manchandani's staff and carried away towards his SUV. Manchandani then got up in a hurry and shook Dhruv's hand.

'Pardon me, Dhruv, but I'll have to take your leave.'

But Dhruv stopped him in his track and said, 'Mr Manchandani, there seems to be an issue with the cheque. It hasn't been cleared yet.'

'Are you sure, Dhruv? Because your uncle and your

cousin had personally collected the same from me,' he said, impatiently looking at the ticking clock in front. 'Listen, that's hardly a problem... Srinivasan!' he called out loud.

On Srinivasan's arrival, Manchandani introduced him to Dhruv. 'Dhruv, he heads our accounts. You can take it up with him. He will furnish all the details. Phew... I wish I could spend more time with you, but kindly excuse me. I have a flight to catch.'

He shook Dhruv's hand and ordered his employee to check-in the consignment as he took leave.

Srinivasan assured Dhruv that the payment had been made, but Dhruv insisted that he had checked up with his bank and that the money hadn't been credited. Srinivasan then dipped into his files and browsed his computer records.

'We have over a thousand clients and vendors, Sir. A very long list indeed,' Srinivasan told Dhruv, while going through the records. Dhruv nodded, waiting patiently. He took a couple of deep breaths to calm down, hoping that all would be well.

'What's the name of your company, Sir?' Srinivasan asked.

'The Alchemists,' Dhruv replied.

Srinivasan punched in 'The Alchemists' but found no records. 'I don't see any transactions with The Alchemists, Mr Dhruv,' he said.

Dhruv wondered what had happened, and said, 'See, I was telling you that my account hasn't been cleared.'

Srinivasan wore a puzzled look and after deliberating for half a minute, he said, 'But your uncle and cousin had personally come over and they sat with me to get your company registered. How is it not showing up then? Why don't you call him up?'

Dhruv was getting worried with every passing second. He said, 'He isn't taking calls right now.'

'But he spoke to one of our employees the other day, confirming that you'll give us the material today,' said Mr Srinivasan.

'What? Are you sure?' asked Dhruv, astonished.

Srinivasan rang a bell to call one of his associates who confirmed the same. Dhruv still couldn't connect the dots. The father-son duo was certainly up to something. Srinivasan continued browsing through the transaction list and he finally found something.

'There you go, Mr Dhruv, just found out the cheque details. It was issued on the fourth of this month, in the name of Vidur & Sons Pvt Ltd,' he said, reading closely from the monitor.

'What?' Dhruv was aghast. Vidur & Sons Pvt Ltd! The name itself was a blow. Dhruv was freaking out and a sense of insecurity began gripping him tightly.

'Are you…are you sure?' he asked hesitantly.

Srinivasan punched a couple of keys and before Dhruv could say anything further, the printer placed on the next table started whirring. A couple of lights flashed and out came the hard copy of the company and transaction details. Srinivasan handed over the sheet to Dhruv.

As he began reading it, a chill ran down his spine.

Company	:	Vidur & Sons Pvt Ltd.
Address	:	16/7 Tagore Street, Banaras–221002
Bank	:	Bank of Banaras
Account No.	:	03860044871

It was the address of Vidur's rented house, and the same

bank and same branch as that of The Alchemists.

The shocking details chilled the marrow within Dhruv's bones. He was duped very badly.

'Sir, we just checked up with the bank. Vidur & Sons had received the funds four days back,' said Srinivasan.

This had been in the making since a long time, realized Dhruv. The incident when he had caught Rishi red-handed flashed across his mind. Vidur always had an inferiority complex due to his father, who had ousted him from the business because of his incompetence. It was all falling in place and the dots were connecting. Dhruv began sweating profusely. He couldn't believe that his entire company was falling apart right before his eyes.

Collecting himself, he told Srinivasan, 'Listen Mr Srinivasan, there is some massive confusion. Our company's name is The Alchemists. So, kindly, just do the necessary amendment.'

'Sir, the company was registered by your trusted partner, your uncle. The amount has been duly cleared, the material received and dispatched with Mr Manchandani. The transaction has been completed from our end,' he replied.

Dhruv was losing his patience as he said, 'Listen, there is some massive fraud or error. Please understand this, I'll be ruined. I have put in everything I had to buy the material for this consignment. Please...'

Srinivasan patiently heard him out and then said, 'Sir, I can't really help you out with this. You have to sort it out with Mr Vidur. I am just an accountant, but honestly even Mr Manchandani won't help you with this. You have my sympathies but please understand, we've made the payment.'

Dhruv packed his stuff and immediately left for Banaras.

Without wasting a minute, he rushed straight to his office. A gamut of emotions had engulfed him. He was a raging bull and a wounded tiger at the same time. Buoyed by fury and bogged down by anxiety, his dichotomy was palpable as he walked into his office. He called Rishi and his uncle. They weren't there. The office staff told him that they hadn't come for days. A furious Dhruv sent one of them over to Vidur's house.

Dhruv, meanwhile, called over his attorney to explore his legal options. He was trying hard to muster courage even though he was completely shattered. A legal notice was soon sent to Vidur and Rishi. Dhruv's attorney told him that their case wasn't really watertight. The furrows on Dhruv's forehead began deepening with worry. Most of his savings had gone into purchasing the precious gems for his clients in Delhi. He was finding it difficult to meet the running expenses of the company. It was a colossal loss.

'Dhruv don't forget, Vidur and Rishi are also partners in The Alchemists. The legal battle will be for the rights to the company as well,' said the attorney.

'And remember if we don't get this money, there will be no company left,' he said remorsefully.

The exchange of legal letters and notices continued. One such day, a lonely Dhruv walked out towards the ghats, introspecting about the happenings in his life. He was sitting on one of the steps, lost in thought, gazing at the star-studded sky when he heard someone call out his name. It was the priest.

Turning around, Dhruv looked at him and in an uncharacteristically jaded voice, he said, 'I am tired...really tired.'

The Miscarriage of Trust

The priest, though, generally abrasive, was slightly restrained and in a mellow tone, he said, 'You're not tired, you cannot be... You are not like others, are you?'

Dhruv smiled and said, 'You know, my Baba, my teachers, friends—everyone would always say, "Dhruv, you're not like others. You're special. You're ahead of the curve...star... wonder child...golden boy...prodigy..." God!' Dhruv broke down while speaking.

'Didn't know you were one to cry at the drop of a hat,' the priest quipped, trying to lighten the moment.

'I am a star in this also,' Dhruv said, chuckling through his tears.

The priest sat down next to him and said, 'I am sure you've heard the cliché "Tough times don't last; tough people do"?'

'Beaten to death,' said Dhruv.

'I know, I am telling you this because it is total crap, not true. Truth is, neither tough men, nor tough times— nothing lasts forever,' he said. 'Nothing lasts forever, Dhruv,' he repeated solemnly.

'Then what the hell are we doing things for?' Dhruv instinctively replied.

The repartee was such that the priest broke into peals of laughter. Dhruv too started laughing. Catching his breath, the priest said, 'That's something you've got to figure out and I know, you will one day. A day will indeed come when the dots will connect and you'll know what the hell you're here to do.' He laughed at the last words again. 'Woah, you're a tough cookie, Dhruv. Never ever say that you're tired again. You have a long way to go,' he almost prophesied.

The conversation and the philosophical exchange

continued till late in the night. After a while, the priest dozed off, chanting hymns. Dhruv, however, was wide awake. Amidst all the worries and emotional entanglements, Dhruv couldn't sleep a wink. In the calm of the night, he took a long walk along the ghats. It was all silent, a rarity in the vibrant city of Banaras. He could see people sleeping by the roadside on the ghats, curled up with their scarce belongings at times. Some had tied their bicycles and rickshaws to trees. Truck drivers were snoring in the confines of their vehicles. As Dhruv passed by each of them, he felt as if he was passing by narratives and stories rather than men and women. Narratives so complex, so vivid and yet so similar, as each one of them had one thing in common—a quest. The quest for food, money, health or prosperity and that too when they also knew that nothing lasts forever.

As Dhruv kept walking and passing by these vivid narratives, he came across a little homeless boy who wore a beaming smile. The boy was exuberantly jumping around the ghat. He would walk down the ghat, touch the water, laugh out loud and come back again. At two o'clock in the morning, this little kid seemed to be having the time of his life. An intrigued Dhruv stopped by and asked the child, 'What's your name, kid?'

The kid smiled and in a shy yet audible tone, he said, 'Yash', which means fame.

'Okay, Yash, what are you doing this late in the night?'

A shy Yash didn't answer and chuckled. Dhruv curiously asked him again, 'Why are you touching the water again and again?'

Yash shook his head and said, 'No, no, no! I am not touching the water.'

The Miscarriage of Trust

'Then what?' asked Dhruv.

'My Baba tells me that I'll one day touch the stars. I think today is that day. Come, I'll show you.'

The little kid excitedly grabbed Dhruv's finger and took him near the water. 'There, you see the stars,' he laughed again and lovingly touched the reflection of the star-studded sky in the water. 'Do you also want to touch the stars?' he innocently asked Dhruv.

Dhruv gently ruffled the kid's hair and said, 'Yes.'

Dhruv looked down on the water as an echo of his childhood played in his mind. 'Dhruv one day you'll be amongst the stars,' he remembered his Baba's almost prophetic assertion. Dhruv gently touched the reflection of the stars.

The little child's gesture had so many layers to it. *Touching the stars—was it a reality or an illusion or perhaps both?*, he wondered.

As the ripened night was giving way to the first break of dawn, in another part of the world the night was still young. Amidst loud music, dance and celebratory drinks in the party lounge of a Swiss hotel, Emma walked out and headed straight towards her room. She seemed to be having some trouble with her eyeliner and make-up. She had a tissue in her hand and was seen constantly rubbing her eyes. Maintaining a seemingly pleasant smile, she greeted all the people she met through the lobby and up the staircase. She was finally relieved to reach the room, which she immediately locked from inside. She literally dragged herself till the dressing table and on the big mirror in front, she saw her face. Her hair was a little undone, the eyeliner a bit messed up, and right under her eye there was a bluish mark, which had swollen up. It was painful as a jittery Emma started crying. She was trembling with fear as her phone rang. Nick was calling her up again and again and then she heard a voice message from him, which said, 'Now don't overreact Emma, it was just a reflex action. Big deal. Now come down immediately. All guests are waiting. Do not—I repeat—do not make it awkward.'

A docile Emma was feeling suffocated and threatened to a point where she broke down.

Nick was an absolute animal, she realized. They had been married for less than a month, yet Emma had realized that Nick wasn't the person she thought he was. His often-ignored eccentricities were actually streaks of his underlying dark side. As Emma was trying to calm her nerves and nurse her injury, she heard thunderous knocking on the door.

'Open the door!' Nick shouted from the other end, followed by some more thunderous knocking. Every knock was like a bolt striking Emma's already weakened heart. She was scared to the core and with a trembling hand, she opened the door. Nick was fuming. A defensive Emma stepped back and started fumbling for words. Nick took a couple of steps towards her and just when it seemed that he would do the untoward, he seemed to turn over a new leaf. 'Baby, I hurt you. I'm a freak. You should slap me back... slap me back.' He grabbed Emma's shivering hand and started slapping himself with it repeatedly.

Emma's psyche was getting disturbed watching Nick behave strangely. She tried to catch her breath. Nick meanwhile had started crying. His emotional instability and explosive outbursts were a scary sight.

'Have you forgiven me? Please forgive me,' he pleaded, falling on Emma's feet.

'Yes... Yes...' said Emma, trying to keep a distance. She

was so anxious that she almost broke down again.

Nick collected himself, looked at her face and said, 'Come down immediately. People are waiting for us, do you get that?'

Emma remained silent and in a bid to avoid confrontation, she gently nodded, as Nick left. Emma had always been a cheerful girl, full of life, the kind who would even smile through difficult times by counting her blessings. This simple girl never had the stomach for conflict, or to fight and shout back at people. She was unnerved and shocked by the absolute brazenness with which she was being treated. That night, with her head buried in the pillow, she cried her heart out. With every rolling tear, a number of thoughts crossed her mind.

In the first few days after marriage, Nick seemed to be a doting husband in love with her, but eventually his basal self came to the fore. Emma thought over it through the night. She wanted someone's counsel. Dhruv's name popped up in her head, but then she dropped that idea as it could potentially complicate the matter. The next morning she went to her own house, which was now permanently inhabited by her parents. Sugar-coated and sly, her parasite-like parents were having the time of their lives. With Emma posted in India, they had the entire house to themselves.

'My love, you look so pretty,' said Emma's mother, as she hugged her. 'Look at you, all married and nice but you've lost a lot of weight. We've been missing you so much,' she said.

'Why didn't you both come to the wedding then?' Emma asked. A tinge of disappointment was apparent in her voice.

'Uh... Uh...' fumbling for words, Marla said, 'Oh my love, we curse ourselves every day for that. It was just that your father wasn't feeling that well and I have this flight-phobia, where I dread being in the air for long. But it's our mistake, we should have come. After all, it was our little girl's big day.' She kissed Emma's forehead.

The niceties continued through the day as an anxious Emma saw the clock ticking by. She and Nick were supposed to leave for India the next day. Her anxiety kept escalating and as it assumed epic proportions, she decided to confide in her mother.

'How is our son-in law?' asked Marla.

Emma kept quiet for a second and then she got up gingerly and sat her mother down for a talk. 'Listen mother, I am really confused. I mean, I don't know how to explain this,' Emma broke down as she tried to speak. Marla showed her a bit of concern and asked her what had happened.

'Mother, Nick is a strange man. He was earlier very loving and nice. I wasn't sure about marriage, but then he proposed and kept wooing me. We got married but ever since then, he has been weird, impulsive and at times…at times even violent.' Emma broke down again and hugged her mother. 'I… I don't feel like going to India with him. I just don't feel safe,' she said, sounding extremely vulnerable.

Marla got a little worried for herself. She and Jamie had the time of their lives in Emma's absence. Their splurging and freedom would be curtailed if Emma decided to stay back.

'Emma, my sweetheart, let me tell you something as a mother today. Marriage is a compromise, my love. There is nothing like a perfect marriage. You have to work towards a successful marriage,' she counselled, keeping her own interests in mind.

'But mother, I feel uneasy when he is around me and he gets physically violent,' Emma confided.

'Emma, my love, it takes time for things to settle down.

You can't just abandon a marriage so quickly, without even working on it. Tomorrow, you'll feel guilty about taking a hasty call. So, sweetheart, go to India with Nick. You both work your respective jobs and things are going to get better,' she said.

After thinking long and hard over it, Emma did finally decide to leave for India with Nick. However, she was apprehensive and nervous. She tried to engage with Nick in a bid to normalize the relation. Deprived of love all her life, she really wanted things to work out. Seated in the flight, she looked out through the window at the setting sun. A part of her didn't want to go. It just didn't feel right to her. A little support from parents would have perhaps held her back but destiny had something else in store. The plane took off for India, the land with which Emma had a special connection. Fascinated with the country since childhood, Emma at times wondered how life always took her there, where she felt a distinct sense of absolution.

Chapter 14

The Cornered Warrior

Case No. 412/C/0587: Ownership dispute
Applicant: Dhruv Samrat

The file was placed on the judge's desk in the Banaras district court. Dhruv was present with his attorney by his side. So were Vidur and Rishi with their counsel. The hearings were a painful process for Dhruv who had to exercise a lot of restraint during the explosive discussion. The proceedings had been going on for some time and a conclusion seemed round the corner. Things seemed a bit bleak for Dhruv. Even though he had a strong claim over his business, the fact that there wouldn't be much left of it if he didn't get back the siphoned amount, gave him sleepless nights. All his resources had dried up and he had his back to the wall. It wasn't just the business ownership case that was keeping him awake, a verdict was also soon expected in the script copyright case that he had grown tired of fighting against Zubin Mistry in Mumbai.

As was his habit, Dhruv picked up a pen and addressed his thoughts to Emma.

Dear Emma,

You'll probably never read what I am writing. I always thought that one day, I'll sit with you and watch you read how much I missed you all these days. We would smile about it, cherish it as a memory and never ever leave each other again. Alas! That day will never come. I just hope that you're happy and smiling wherever you are. But then, I am going to continue writing to you, because that is the only catharsis my soul yearns for. You know, Emma, the one thing that I take solace in, is that you're happy and smiling. For me, that glint in your green eyes when you smile is the most precious thing on earth. As for me, I will survive and live to fight another day, I guess.

However, the truth was that Emma was far from happiness and marital bliss. She was reduced to a pale shadow of her former self. Nick's crazy antics and aggressive obstinacy had slowly turned an otherwise vibrant Emma into a quiet, listless woman, grappling with life. Even during the most tumultuous times, she had never slipped into such a cocoon. She would barely speak at work. Her colleagues had also noticed a radical change in her demeanour. Nick had transformed Emma into a trophy wife, which he had perhaps always wanted.

One afternoon, she received a call. It was Dhruv.

'Hi Dhruv...' she said. Her voice lacked the spunk characteristic to her personality. Dhruv felt a little strange.

'Emma... Emma, are you comfortable speaking or should I call later?' he asked gently.

'No, Dhruv, it's okay. I can talk,' she said glumly.

'Okay... How is life post marriage?' he asked playfully.

'It's fine,' she replied with a straight face.

Dhruv could sense the underlying stress and tension in her voice. He paused for a second and then said, 'Emma, what's the problem?'

Emma cleared her throat and said, 'Nothing...'

Her voice seemed a bit shaky and a few moments later, it totally gave in to the emotional onslaught she was braving.

'Emma! Emma!' Dhruv shouted from the other end as Emma broke down. 'What happened?' he frantically asked. His heart sank every time he heard her cry.

'Nothing, Dhruv, nothing. It's just that I am trying to adapt to marriage. You know, it's not a big deal...pretty normal with married couples,' she said.

'That's bull crap, Emma.'

Emma broke down again, despite trying hard to cover up her emotional vulnerability.

'Emma, I am coming to see you, okay?' he said, assuring her.

'No, Dhruv, it's fine. Your coming might complicate things,' she replied.

'I can't see or hear you like this,' he said, freaking out.

Emma tried to persuade Dhruv against coming to Delhi. However, he was too disturbed to hear an otherwise eternally cheerful Emma breaking down so inconsolably.

Emma's husband Nick seemed to have a strange kind of split personality. He was extremely warm, cordial and gentlemanly with friends and acquaintances at social gatherings. He would treat Emma like a princess in front of them. However, his inner beast was reserved for her in the confines of the four walls of their home. Even in the precincts of his privacy, he had mood fluctuations, swinging from being highly caring and affectionate, to being extremely indignant, to, at times, being even violently aggressive.

A couple of days after Dhruv had spoken to Emma over the phone, he arrived in New Delhi. He had myriad personal problems to deal with. However, they weren't a patch on how disturbed he was with regards to Emma's turmoil. Around seven in the evening, he reached the Swiss Embassy to see her. He was guided to her house inside the Embassy. The apartments seemed lively and buzzing with activity as a social get-together was underway. Dhruv looked around for Emma and then what he saw, stirred him to the core. Emma was reduced to a pale shadow of herself. She had lost a lot of weight. The spunk, the charm, had all faded away. She seemed totally languid as she nodded to the conversations around. Amidst the social formalities, she saw Dhruv standing at the door. A smile blossomed on her face. It was a testimony to the magical connection the two shared, where they could make the other smile or laugh at a time when they had their backs to the wall.

As Emma looked on towards Dhruv, she felt a magnetic pull as her steps took her in that direction. It had been long since she had seen or met anyone of her own during this tumultuous phase. Her eyes began welling up with every single step and as she reached the door, she just broke down and hugged Dhruv. For that moment, she didn't care about the onlookers, the social stigma. It was just an expression of relief for a suffocated soul who had worn a dignified silence on the outside but was shouting for help deep inside.

Nick wasn't too happy to see Dhruv. However, as he was very careful about his public image, he graciously welcomed

Dhruv and even raised a toast to him. While doing so, he asked Dhruv and Emma to join him by his side. He grabbed Emma by the shoulder, his nails digging deep into her skin and a plastic smile adorning his face. Emma was getting hurt. Dhruv's eyes were quick to notice Nick's savageness. Dhruv was livid. He tapped Nick's arm forcefully, camouflaging it as a hug to maintain social formalities.

'Dhruv, you should not have come and done what you did,' said Emma.

Dhruv shook her and said, 'Emma, are you mad? Look at yourself—this is not the Emma I've known. This guy is an animal alright! You can't be staying with him! What's wrong with you?'

Emma gave a wry smile laced with melancholy. She said, 'Exactly what's wrong with me, I sometimes wonder. There must be something wrong with me, which is why my parents abandoned me at birth. In fact, there must be something really wrong, which is why you too left me.'

Dhruv's heart plummeted to an abyss as he heard this. He felt pained to have hurt her unintentionally.

'And surely there must be something terribly wrong with me that now my husband turns into an animal when he is around me.' A distraught Emma felt choked with emotion, as she broke down. Dhruv was heartbroken to see her in this state. He was devastated to know the kind of questions and complexities an affection-hungry Emma was grappling with on a daily basis. He hugged her and said, 'Nothing is wrong with you Emma… Never ever say that again… It's just that the world is not good enough for you.'

The Cornered Warrior

Dhruv then affectionately kissed her on her forehead and said, 'What's with your weight? You've lost a lot. It's almost scary. You've got to take care.'

Emma brushed it aside and said, 'There is a lot to take care of.'

'Emma, you can't stay with this man. He is destroying your very essence, and do you get that?' he almost begged.

'Dhruv, I want to be absolutely sure before I pull the plug on this relationship.' She smiled and in a sad voice, said, 'One thing I am going to carry to my grave is a clean conscience. I should never have the regret that I didn't do my bit to make things work.'

Dhruv was struck by the sheer piousness of Emma's thoughts. She was a pure soul—a fact Dhruv had known for a long time. 'Emma, you don't get it. It's a mean, crazy world out there, ready to take you on. There is no place for goodness in this world,' he said.

Emma patiently heard him out. She took a deep breath and said, 'Dhruv, I never say this, but now I have to I guess—the world is a mean, nasty place...' she said, repeating Dhruv's words. 'You know how many times that thought flashes across a little girl's mind while growing up in an orphanage without knowing who her parents are?'

Dhruv nodded in empathy.

'Every day—every single day! But I never believed in that thought. Not once... Because I've always had this indomitable belief in the creed of goodness, in the creed of gratitude for one's blessings.'

'It's all about smelling the roses,' Dhruv remembered.

'The only time I actually, for a short while, believed that the world is a mean place was when we broke up. And don't get me wrong, Dhruv, I don't blame you for it.'

Dhruv was devastated and pained to hear that.

'I lost faith for a short while that day, because here we had two people who both loved each other and wanted to be together, but alas! The universe conspired to keep them away.' Tears began rolling down from her eyes.

A heartbroken Dhruv wanted to tell her how much he still loved her. He was yearning to tell her about how a few months back, he had come to the embassy to ask for her hand, only to learn about Nick's arrival in her life. But just like that day, Dhruv bit his lips and hugged her.

'Emma…just take care and stay safe. And listen, no matter what, I am just a phone call away,' he said.

The two were about to take each other's leave when suddenly Nick stormed towards the lobby area where they were standing. It was just the three of them there. Nick was fuming. His maniacal streak was in full display as he charged towards Emma. Dhruv feared for her and tried to calmly pacify him.

'Will you stay out of it, Dhruv!' he shouted, pushing Dhruv aside in a rather rough fashion. Nick then caught hold of Emma by her shoulder. 'Why did you have to make a fool of me there? Why God dammit?' he shouted out loud in a fit of fury.

'Behave yourself, Nick!' she said.

'Really, you think I need to behave myself?' He started grinning sarcastically.

Dhruv, meanwhile, fearing for Emma's safety, started apologizing to Nick. 'Nick, I am really sorry if you got offended by my coming over. Trust me, Emma hadn't called me. I just came over uninvited.'

The Cornered Warrior

Nick didn't say a word. He just kept pacing up and down the lobby. His violent behaviour and unnerving silence were freaking out both Emma and Dhruv. After a minute, the venom spilled out. 'You've slept with him, right?' he asked Emma. 'How many times have you slept with him, Emma?'

Dhruv was livid. 'Nick, you are crossing—'

'Just shut up and get lost, will you!' Nick shouted him down.

Nick then turned back to Emma and asked her again, 'Tell me, how was he in bed? Tell me!'

Before Dhruv could say another word, Emma asked Dhruv to leave immediately.

'You get lost!' shouted Nick, pushing him again.

A teary-eyed Dhruv didn't want to leave Emma alone. He didn't mind the insults being hurled at him as much as he feared for Emma's well-being.

'Just leave, Dhruv… Just leave,' insisted Emma.

Dhruv reluctantly started moving towards the exit of the lobby. He looked back one final time to see a visibly tensed Emma, painfully thin and frail, hounded by a beast of a man. It was a sight that would haunt him for months together.

A disillusioned Dhruv was finding it difficult to come to terms with his predicament. One after the other, things were falling apart. The legal proceedings and the lack of funds for his business had pushed him to the wall. Dhruv knew that he had been a fighter since birth. He had wrestled with debts, deaths and financial woes in the past as well. However, this time it was different. Emma's perplexed and listless look from that day had scarred his mind. He was just not able to focus on anything. And then one day came a bombshell announcement. Dhruv Samrat had lost the copyright case to film-maker Zubin Mistry. It was heartbreaking for Dhruv. He could not prove that the story was his creation. It was officially attributed to Zubin's fiancée who didn't know a thing about storytelling and writing. The temporary stay on the film's release was also removed. Amidst fanfare and media blitz, the film was released. Dhruv only got a passing mention as 'a cheap publicity-craving struggler' by one newspaper.

Dear Emma,

I hope you're doing well. Today is a big day of my life. My film got released finally. Oh yes, I can say 'my film' to you at least, because you know that's the truth. Others might call me a fraud, a wannabe or even a cheap publicity-seeker. Even though I knew it's not going to do me any good to go and watch this film, I did actually buy a ticket.

As the credits rolled and I saw someone else's name under 'Written by,' I felt numb. It was a feeling of nothingness that I'll never forget in my life. Little did I know that this was just the beginning. As the movie unfolded, I saw scene after scene pan out precisely the way I had envisioned. The audience was laughing, crying and even clapping at precisely the moments I had guessed they would do while writing the scenes. The most brutal irony was that once when I didn't clap during a scene, the person sitting next to me got offended and gave me a cold stare. He would have mocked me to death had I told him that I had written that scene. As I was coming out of the theatre, I heard people talk amongst themselves. I think they loved the film... It could have been the most successful day of my life but alas! It turned out to be the most haunting failure. Perhaps the title of my story, The Most Successful Failure, was indeed prophetic!

Dhruv's pen stopped with an exclamation mark as he lay down to rest.

Salvation lies within—Dhruv's message from his story echoed across the chambers of his mind all night. He maintained a low profile for the next few days. His business was running out of funds. He was trying hard to salvage what he could. Vidur and Rishi had ripped him off thousands of rupees. The legal case was in its final stages. Dhruv walked around his office. Looking at the title board—The Alchemists—he wondered the significance of the word in his life. An old memory from his childhood flashed across his mind. Dhruv's Baba used to tell him that their forefathers were alchemists, who could transform lead into gold as per the village folklore.

That night he sat down with the priest at his modest, makeshift straw hut along the ghats.

'You know, when I was a little boy, I once told my Baba rather excitedly, that I'll grow up and became an alchemist. He would dismiss the idea and ask me to do my own thing,' he said, reminiscing about his conversations with his father. 'But the word "alchemist" hasn't left me since then. It keeps coming to me naturally, whether it was while narrating my script to Zubin or renaming our business. I wonder why…' he asked.

The priest carefully heard him and said, 'You know, your father came to me once to talk about it, when you were small.'

'Really?' asked Dhruv.

'Yes, the entire village and, in fact, parts of the city had heard stories about your alchemist forefathers. Some said that they had mystical powers, some called them crazy. Nobody really knows, but the truth is that they kept striving all their lives, right till their death.'

'That's why Baba never really wanted me to be a part of this mystical world of gems, stones and alchemy,' he said.

The priest had a hearty laugh and said, 'It doesn't work like this, does it, Dhruv? Wants and desires—not all of them get fulfilled.'

'Yes, but Baba did keep me away from alchemy. I'll never be an alchemist. I don't even know much about it and I don't even know whether it is really true in the first place.'

'Never say never, Dhruv,' the priest smiled.

'Listen, you're losing it. You mean, I can be an alchemist who transforms lead into gold. Are you smoking something, I don't know!' he said.

The priest continued laughing and said, 'All I am saying is, never say never.'

'I think you need to sleep. I'll go,' Dhruv said.

'Yes, and you need to wake up,' the priest winked as Dhruv walked away.

Dhruv was trying his best to put up a brave front. However, deep inside, he was breaking down with every passing day. Everything was falling apart one after the other, and in his battle, he was all alone.

The next day was the final hearing of the case between Dhruv and Vidur for the ownership of the business. Dhruv was standing in the witness box and with due permission from the judge, he spoke out. At this emotionally vulnerable moment, Dhruv didn't really weigh his words and spoke from the heart.

'My Lord, and members of the house, I must tell you today

that the business we are talking about, named "The Alchemists", was officially started by my father, even though its roots can be traced back to the generations before. My father had named it "Samrat Stones and Pearls". After my father's demise, I renamed it The Alchemists. It is an ode to my forefathers, who the village folk believed were alchemists—or should we say, men with mystical powers who could transform ordinary lead into gold. To some, it may sound like fiction, but to me, it always had a deeper meaning. Maybe transforming ordinary metal to precious gold had metaphorical connotations that we are not able to comprehend today. Who knows? But the bottom line is that, for us, this was always a holy and spiritual pursuit rather than just a money-making enterprise. My uncle, Vidur, is the complete antithesis of this legacy. Fifteen years back, my father saw him struggling in our business. Mr Vidur's incompetence and lack of transparency were palpable. However, being a loving brother, he helped Mr Vidur open a business of his own, across the river. Unfortunately, he didn't mend his ways. But then years later, after my father's death, at a tough and lonely moment, I trusted him again. I was wrong. He siphoned off funds and opened a parallel company named "Vidur & Sons", Dhruv wore a wry smile.

'The man was clear in his head. He didn't come here to help me build this company. All he wanted was to rip me off. Your Honour, I am an artist, I am not an entrepreneur. I joined this business because I had creditors breathing down my neck. When my father died, I made a promise to myself that I am going to pay every single penny he ever owed. And I lived up to my words. Wherever my Baba is, he is surely relieved and smiling. He never wanted me in this business, but it's been an enriching experience for me to know about gems, stones and their rather mystical powers, and that is something none can take away from me. I realized that whether it is art, business or any vocation, their grammar might differ but the essence remains the same—the essence of passion, intent and resolve. Unfortunately, my partner, Mr Vidur, and his son, Rishi, don't share that view.'

Dhruv then looked towards them and said, 'Yes, you might siphon off money today and earn a quick buck, but you'll never be able to build a business or a company because you don't have it in you to do that.' Dhruv very eloquently continued, 'Once a fraud, always a fraud, Your Honour. The Alchemists has a different DNA. Your Honour, today I fear absolutely nothing. And that's because, irrespective of your judgement, if there is one thing that the last few years have taught me, it is that I will survive.'

'I will survive!' he repeated passionately. 'I have survived family deaths, treason, debts, theft, heartbreak, loss and what not. I've only gotten stronger and wiser.'

Dhruv's words spoke volumes about his character. The starry-eyed little boy from Banaras, who grew up without a mother, had withstood the rigours of life to evolve into a wise man who was today bruised and scarred but stronger nevertheless. Vidur and Rishi were thoroughly shamed by Dhruv, who spoke his heart out that day. However, he knew as well as anyone else that in a court of law, a fiery speech and intention, have little bearing on the judgement.

And finally the moment came. The judge pronounced the decision. He quoted various sections under law and also cited from previous judgements. He then remarked, 'Dhruv Samrat, you've had a pretty hard journey and you've done well post your father's death to pay off every penny of debt he owed.

Your father must be proud of you. The court announces that Dhruv Samrat, son of Ram Samrat, reserves all rights to The Alchemists.' Dhruv sighed in relief, but his happiness was short-lived, as the judge continued, 'However, the charges of embezzlement of funds against Mr Vidur and Mr Rishi cannot be proved due to paucity of evidence.' Vidur and Rishi wore a wry smile on hearing that.

Though his uncle and cousin had siphoned off major funds from the company, leaving it lifeless, they could not steal the soul of The Alchemists from Dhruv, for whom it was a bittersweet judgement. It was a moral vindication for Dhruv, though he had lost nearly all his money and resources. The Alchemists was reduced to a signboard bereft of stones, jewels, artisans and employees. As the court proceedings came to an end and the people dispersed, Dhruv saw Vidur and Rishi standing right in front. As their eyes locked, Dhruv's resolute gaze exuded his indomitable spirit. It had the belief and the hunger of starting again from scratch; it also had piercing honesty, something that shamed Vidur so much that he lowered his eyes.

Dhruv was looking to usher a new beginning in his life.

Chapter 15

The Abode of Death

The next morning, Dhruv woke up before the first rays of the sun had hit the ghats. Someone was playing a melodious flute nearby. The chirping of the birds and the cool breeze coming through the window of his room acted like a balm on his bruised mind. However, as he got up that morning, he felt a huge weight lift off his shoulders. The burden of debts and legal cases was replaced by the lightness and exuberance of a beginner. As he laced up his shoes and began sprinting outside, he felt a surge of relief and rejuvenation in his heart. The doubts, dilemmas and conflicts seemed to have been replaced by hope, belief and willpower.

A barrage of thoughts continued flooding his mind as he picked his pace and lengthened his strides. The Alchemists still belonged to him and what also belonged to him was his unrelenting spirit, which had survived the onslaught of time. There was so much to do and look forward to, he thought, and then what flashed across his mind was Emma's visual. Her confused and disillusioned look caused a lump in his throat. He stopped to catch a breath.

He then walked a couple of steps down the Dashashwamedha Ghat and bent to collect a handful of holy water. Rolling up his sleeves, he washed his face and forearms. And then with a prayer for Emma on his lips, he poured the holy water from his cupped hands, bowing down before the golden rays of the sun.

'Dhruv... Dhruv...' he heard his name. He looked around. There was no one. Dhruv closed his eyes and prayed again. Immersed thus, he felt a nudge on his shoulder. He turned around, but there was no one. It was Emma's touch he sensed. He felt a sort of telepathic connection with her. A curious Dhruv started getting worried for her. He had an intuition that Emma was asking for help. The worry soon escalated to anxiety, and before Dhruv knew it, his anxiety snowballed into panic. He called up Emma. Nobody took the call.

Nothing seemed right to Dhruv. It had been two months since that horrific night when Emma and Nick had a showdown. Dhruv didn't want to complicate matters and had, hence, refrained from giving in to the urge of going to Delhi to see her. A few days later, Dhruv tried reaching out to her again. However, the number didn't connect. He searched his records and diaries, trying hard to look for a common connection, but nothing came up. He kept searching and browsing through his folders and card holder. He finally found Emma's Swiss landline number. He called up, but to his surprise, he found out that Emma wasn't there either. Her parents seemed least bothered about her whereabouts. Dhruv then called up the Swiss Embassy to enquire about her. The receptionist initially didn't entertain Dhruv's queries. However, after much persuasion, she told Dhruv that Emma had left the job about a month back.

Dhruv's fears were getting compounded with every passing day. He wanted to leave his number at the desk and requested the receptionist to inform him in case she received any more information about Emma. The lady, however, politely refused, citing that more information, even if available, would be only shared with a family member.

He dialled Emma's Swiss landline number again. It was answered by her mother. A nervous Dhruv again enquired about Emma's whereabouts, but her mother didn't have a clue, and neither was she interested. Dhruv voiced his concern about her troubled marriage and her unknown whereabouts. However, Emma's mother, Marla, didn't break a sweat on hearing that. She was too preoccupied with her own world, enjoying the luxuries given to her by her daughter who was nowhere to be found. A disillusioned Dhruv hung up and pondered for a while. The lady's insensitivity made his heart go out to Emma. She had been a wonderful daughter to worthless parents who had abandoned her at birth and were now least thankful or worried about their daughter, an apostle of selfless love, who always believed in the creed of giving.

Dhruv continued trying to connect to other people. However, it was all in vain. He finally packed his bags and decided to leave for Delhi. He was determined to get to Emma. He feared for her safety, he feared for her health. She was a delicate, soft-hearted girl, who was too pure for the big, bad, ugly world.

The long train journey seemed even longer as a worried Dhruv continued racking his brains to try and figure out Emma's whereabouts. He didn't sleep a wink as the train reached the Nizamuddin Station in the early hours of the morning. Dhruv took an auto and headed straight to the Swiss Embassy. He tried hard to enquire and find out about Emma, but to no avail. A dispirited Dhruv waited for hours before

The Abode of Death

he was finally called in by the senior manager at the High Commission. Dhruv had begged for her attention and finally got the chance to enquire directly from her.

'Mr Dhruv Samrat, you've been calling and enquiring about Emma Schellenberg incessantly,' she said.

'Sorry for troubling you, Madam, but we still don't know where Emma is,' he replied, hopeful yet worried.

'Dhruv, Emma Schellenberg used to work here,' she said.

'That's right,' he acknowledged.

'She left around a month back and since then, we haven't heard from her,' she said, dashing all his hopes.

Dhruv seemed listless for a moment. He sighed out loud in despondency. The lady could sense the sincerity and worry in Dhruv's demeanour.

'Ma'am, you have to help me find her,' he said, folding his hands. 'She...she needs me. And I just know that...' he said, almost on the verge of breaking down.

The lady then said, 'She wasn't doing too well. She had just separated from her husband and then decided to leave.'

'She separated from her husband?' Dhruv wondered out loud, and asked her again.

'Yes, she did. But after that, she just left and didn't really tell anyone where she was going,' she said.

Pursing his lips and thinking hard, Dhruv asked, 'When was her visa going to expire?'

The lady tried hard to remember and said, 'I think she had a few months left.'

'Can you check that?' he asked.

'I will,' she said.

Over the next two to three days, Dhruv searched for her across the city. He visited her favourite places—namely, Lodhi

Garden and India Gate—but he couldn't find her. Dejected and disillusioned, Dhruv sat down helplessly on a bench at India Gate. It was late in the night when Dhruv received a call from an unknown number. He answered the phone and said, 'Hello.' The voice at the other end was surprisingly of the priest from Banaras.

'Priest, is that you?' Dhruv enquired.

'Yes, Dhruv, it's me,' he said in a sombre tone.

'Priest, you have no idea what I am going through,' he said.

Before Dhruv could continue, the priest interjected and said, 'Dhruv, somebody wants to talk to you.'

A moment later, Dhruv heard a familiar voice—a voice he had been longing to hear for what seemed like an eternity... It was Emma's.

'Dhruv...' she said.

A tear rolled down Dhruv's cheek. Heaving a sigh of relief and closing his eyes in prayer, he said, 'Emma... I missed you... I missed you beyond what words can describe.'

Emma laughed and said, 'I want to see you, Dhruv! Now! Immediately!'

'What are you doing in Banaras? How have you been? Why did you disappear?' Dhruv rattled off a volley of questions.

Emma laughed and said, 'Come over. I'll answer all your questions. I've all the time in the world.'

'Yeah right! I learned about your separation. He'll rot in hell, you don't worry,' he said.

'How does it affect me Dhruv...' she said nonchalantly.

'Listen, don't worry, you can always start afresh. This was just a bump along the way. You have a long journey ahead in life,' Dhruv assured her.

'Really?' asked Emma.

'Yes, of course, Emma. I'll come and see you,' he said.

'Dhruv... Dhruv...' Emma paused for a second and then continued, 'Come fast, I'll be waiting for you.'

Dhruv couldn't quite gauge the sudden seriousness in Emma's tone. The priest then took the phone and said, 'Dhruv, you need to be in Banaras now.' With these words, he hung up.

Dhruv felt a sense of urgency. However, the very next moment, he felt he was overthinking and reading too much into it. He was relieved to have heard from Emma, but the sense of impatience in her voice continued playing on his mind. There was no train or bus available at that time but Dhruv wanted to leave for Banaras that very night. He found out that a truck was leaving for Banaras, so he requested the driver, who obliged and allowed him to board.

Sitting in the rear, open end of the truck, atop straw and grass, Dhruv stared through the wilderness of the night. A cool breeze and a sense of serenity made him reflect on many things in life. Dhruv was today a beginner with renewed passion and without any baggage of debt or legal cases. His heart still beat for Emma. In fact, it was beating stronger than ever before. As the journey progressed on highways, through tunnels and over bridges, Dhruv symbolically meandered through the troughs and crests of his and Emma's journey. They had been through a lot. Friendship, love, romance, heartbreak and loss—everything flashed before Dhruv's eyes. As his head became heavy with the weight of dreams and ruminations, he closed his eyes, and in the moment of truth and peace, he whispered in his mind, *I love you and I am not letting you go this time.*

A steady downpour followed those words as if it was a

divine signal from the Gods. As the drops of rain fell on his eyes, Dhruv dreamt of a future together with Emma. He was done staying without her. The torrent of rain outside and the drizzle of emotions within soothed his nerves as the journey continued.

The next morning, Dhruv welcomed the rising sun with the hope and desire of starting a new life. He thanked the truck driver and got down on the street next to the Dashashwamedha Ghat. As his feet touched the ground, it dawned on him that he was just a few steps away from Emma. In that moment, he just knew for sure that he would never let go of her ever again. With a wave of excitement soaring inside, Dhruv ran down the steps towards the priest's place. He had told Dhruv that Emma was there with him. One step at a time, Dhruv descended the stairs, and with a smile adorning his face, he knocked on the priest's door, who opened it. A visibly excited Dhruv hugged and greeted him.

'Where's Emma?' he asked excitedly.

Contrary to Dhruv, the priest wore a grim look. He held Dhruv's hands and asked him to accompany him. Dhruv wasn't able to comprehend what was happening. His excitement, however, was waning by the second.

'Where's she?' he asked again.

The priest didn't reply. Dhruv stopped him in his tracks and asked again, 'Priest, where's she? What's happening here?'

The priest nodded and said, 'Just follow me; I am taking you to her.'

Dhruv kept following the priest, who walked past the ghats across the roads. After walking for a mile or two, they entered the priest's ashram named 'Pran Punya', where sick people voluntarily embraced death. Dhruv was still grappling with what was happening. The priest then stopped him at the door and said 'Act bravely, Dhruv.' With these words, he opened the door and let Dhruv inside his ashram. Dhruv took a couple of steps and looked around. And then his eyes stopped at a visual that would haunt him for the rest of his life. He saw a weak, frail woman lying on the bed. An intravenous drip was supporting her and a medical attendant by her side was monitoring the same. She was in pain and was struggling to keep her eyes open. Dhruv couldn't believe what he was seeing. It was Emma.

The vibrant, feisty girl was reduced to a pale shadow of herself. The bag in his hand dropped and so did he. The priest tried to support him and make him stand up, but he was too devastated to move. Emma, meanwhile, sensed his presence. She slowly opened her eyes. Dhruv saw her gaining consciousness and went up to her. He was breathing heavily.

Emma smiled and said softly, 'Dhruv, I'm not dead, so please don't cry.' She was struggling to form the words, her voice barely audible. However, what was still palpable in her voice was an underlying cheerfulness, which had survived countless emotional and physical challenges. She was still smiling. Dhruv held her hand and said, 'I'm not going to let anything happen to you…no…no… This is not happening.'

Emma smiled peacefully and in a low voice, she said, 'Oh Dhruv…'

She was struggling to get up. The attendant and Dhruv helped her. As she got up, she hugged Dhruv and the two broke down.

'Emma, I'm done staying without you. Totally done. You're not going anywhere ever without me, you promise!' he said.

Emma laughed a little and struggling a bit, she said,

'Dhruv, I'm here, right here with you.'

The two shared a bond as divine as the holy Ganges. The priest and the attendant were both moved to tears.

As Dhruv cuddled Emma, she mustered some strength and said, 'Dhruv...now listen to me carefully. I came to Banaras for a special reason. You know what the priest's ashram stands for?'

Dhruv was heartbroken and was crying piteously. Emma continued, 'Dhruv, don't make this difficult for me. This place stands for the "last stop" before nirvana, right, priest?' she asked.

The priest nodded with sadness writ large on his face.

'Emma, you'll get better. We'll go to the best doctors and get you treated,' Dhruv was begging helplessly, and talking so frantically that his words weren't coherent.

Emma calmly smiled and said, 'Dhruv, I don't have that much time, sweetheart. Liver cirrhosis—advanced stage. In fact, it's spreading real fast. The other organs too are failing. Ah...' she sighed and winced in pain for a moment.

An inconsolable Dhruv was attended to by the priest. Dhruv was so devastated that no words of worldly wisdom meant anything at that moment. He was just not ready to accept this chapter of his and Emma's destinies.

'Priest, do something,' he howled his heart out as Emma rested inside.

'Please... Please... Please... God dammit, please!' Dhruv caught hold of the priest's feet and cried till he went numb. The priest then helped Dhruv get up and gave him some water. Dhruv threw up and started feeling ill. Groaning and

The Abode of Death

crying with pain he said, 'Priest, she is the purest human being I've known. Why is this happening to her…why?' he cried out again. Amidst incessant howls, he kept muttering to himself, 'She has never harmed anyone. All she has done in her entire life is to give love and affection and this is what she gets in return.'

The priest felt miserable. He had no answer. He had seen the little boy born right before his eyes, and then suffer so many losses and heartbreaks. It was a shattering experience.

A few moments later, Dhruv got up and asked the priest and the attendant about further details. Emma's reports and the doctor's prescriptions made it amply clear that Emma was on her last legs.

'Dhruv, she is calling you inside,' said the priest.

As Dhruv was about to enter, the priest held him back for a moment and said, 'There is a reason people come to the Pran Punya ashram. They come here to release everything. Help her to do that, Dhruv.'

Dhruv walked into the room, went straight to Emma and hugged her. It was the warmest hug the two had ever shared. Dhruv then held her hand and said, 'Emma, I swear by the Ganges, there has not been a single day when I've not loved you more than I've loved you the day before.'

Emma heartily laughed at the innocence of the statement and was also moved by Dhruv's words. Dhruv, too, smiled for a second but then held her hand again and said, 'Every single day of me being away from you was a battle. And all that kept me going was the hope that one day, I'll pay off my debts, clear all the cases and come back to ask for your hand.'

Emma kissed him on his cheek and smiled blissfully.

A teary-eyed Dhruv then said, 'Emma, I'll promise you

one thing today—that in these last days, I'll try and be the lover, the friend—the *everything*—you've truly deserved all your life.'

The two then hugged each other for a moment.

'Dhruv...' Emma said, her voice regaining some strength post the glucose drip. 'I'll be back on my feet tomorrow; I am still not that weak. You have to show me Banaras like never before.' She felt cheerful.

Dhruv smiled and said, 'Sure, but haven't you already seen it like never before, Miss Documentary Film-maker?' He gently tapped her on her nose.

Emma nodded and said, 'That's when I saw Banaras through the lens of a camera. This time I want to see it through your eyes, Dhruv. Got it, Mr Storyteller, Mr Philosopher and God-knows-what? Maybe Mr Alchemist?' The two laughed, sharing a light moment.

The next day, Dhruv and Emma embarked on a spectacular journey. It was a journey for moksha—a journey of enlightenment. Emma was in her element. Sharply dressed in smart trousers and a frilly top with her matching bag and glasses, the girl was in no mood for grieving and complaining. For her, it was just another day in her life, which had so much to offer and explore. Though Dhruv sometimes held her hand to help her, the determined girl that Emma was, she mostly helped herself and walked on her own without any support. She was showing tremendous courage.

As the two walked out, Dhruv complimented her by saying, 'You're beautiful, you know that?'

'Yeah, I have heard that before,' she smiled. 'You're a wordsmith, Dhruv. Why don't you say it in a more profound and unique way?' she playfully said.

The Abode of Death

'Alright, challenge accepted,' he said out loud as the two walked around the narrow lanes of the city, which were bustling with life and energy. Dhruv thought for a moment, cleared his throat and then said, 'You're a majestic manifestation of the divinity envisioned by the Almighty in its most aesthetic avatar... Whoa!'

Emma heard him out and after a moment, she said, 'Nice try...'

'Nice try?' he repeated, surprised. 'Is it not good enough?'

'You can do better,' she said.

'Alright Miss Schellenberg, you've no idea who you've woken up today,' he said.

The playful banter between the two continued, as they got on a traditional, horse-drawn buggy, to take a ride around the city.

'Wow, I love this!' she exclaimed.

'I just thought that this would be the next best thing to walking,' Dhruv said.

The two sat down and enjoyed a panoramic view of the city as the majestic horses draped in shades of saffron and white, drew the buggy.

'Oh Dhruv... You know, this, right here, is life. We don't realize it. We just don't realize that life actually happens while we are busy chasing everything else,' she calmly said, resting her head on Dhruv's shoulder.

Dhruv kissed her forehead and said, 'You remember this place, Emma?' Dhruv pointed towards a quaint, traditional building at the end of the street.

'That's the Heritage Hall, right?' she asked. 'Ah...that's where we met for the first time, honey,' she reminisced.

'Oh God! You know, I remember that day so distinctly,'

Dhruv said. 'My play had just gotten over. There were so many people around and yet all I could see was a green-eyed girl, who was wearing a white top with a floral skirt.'

'My my...you remember!' Emma exclaimed.

'Oh yes, sweetheart, I was on a different trajectory then. And then you just disappeared, you remember?'

'I do...but you can't blame me! You were caught up with other things,' she said.

'Yes, and that, perhaps, is the tragedy of my life...' Dhruv sighed. 'But I did come for you, zipping past everything else,' he remembered.

'But then I was in a different room,' she replied ruefully.

'And when I came there, you had left,' he said with emotions seeping from every word.

Emma then wiped off his tears and said, 'And then we finally met.'

Dhruv smiled and said, 'We did... We did finally meet.'

Thus, Dhruv and Emma fondly remembered their first rendezvous. Little did they know that in the mystique of their first meeting lay a cue about how their lives would unfold.

The two explored all the streets and then stopped by for two of Emma's favourite Banaras delicacies—the Banarasi paan and the kulhad tea. She relished the paan with gay abandon and as the two sat down along the steps of the Assi Ghat sipping the tea, they chatted their hearts out. It had been long since they had had a heart-to-heart discussion.

'Dhruv, I feel so light and alive today. Here we are...no constraints, no stigmas, no boundaries—just the two of us,' she said.

The Abode of Death

Dhruv nodded and said, 'Emma, I want to give you something today.'

'What?' she asked.

Dhruv took out a red diary from his bag—the one that contained all his musings and ramblings addressed to Emma while she wasn't there—and handed it to her.

Emma held it in her hand and asked, 'Dhruv, what's this?'

'Open it and read,' he said.

Emma gently turned the first page of the diary, which had 'Dear Emma' written in bold on top. She began reading.

Dear Emma,

Sometimes I just imagine that you're sitting next to me with a smile adorning your face, lit up beautifully by those prism-like green eyes, through which I wish to view the universe...

Emma was smiling from ear to ear as she affectionately turned the pages.

Dear Emma,

I miss you. I miss the warmth of your touch, the serenity of your presence and the calming assurance of your words.

Emma was already moist-eyed as she continued flipping through the pages.

Dear Emma,

Today I paid off almost all of my father's debts. That day is not very far, Emma...

Page after page, Emma was discovering Dhruv's silent journey towards her. He had not, even for a single day, given up on his love. She continued reading.

Dear Emma,

I wonder what the look on your face would be when I present you this diary someday. I bet you'll be smiling with tears in your eyes, you would be struggling to read it and with a lump in your throat, you'll say, 'I love you, Dhruv,' I hope...

Emma was overwhelmed with Dhruv's words and it took her a minute to absorb everything that she had just read. Taking a deep breath, she said, 'I love you, Dhruv.' The smile on her face was adorned with tears of joy rolling down her blushing cheeks. 'I never knew that you've loved me all this while!' she exclaimed.

As she browsed through another page, it said,

Today, I hope I am able to articulate to you how much I love you. I hope I can hold on to your hand and never let you go...

A touched Emma asked him, 'When was this supposed to be?'

Dhruv laughed at his fate and said, 'This was supposed to be on that day in Delhi, when I came to see you at the Embassy. I was all ready and excited but alas! Before I could say anything, you gave me the news about yourself and Nick.'

Emma closed her eyes and shook her head in despondence.

'That day I thought that that perhaps was a punishment I deserved for letting you down in the past,' he said dejectedly.

Emma held his hand and said, 'Dhruv, look at me and

hear me out carefully. You're one of the purest souls I have ever met in my life. You're the best thing that ever happened to me. Never ever blame yourself for anything. You had lost your father, you had lost your livelihood, there were debts, legal cases… How much can a man take! But you took it all in your stride and tried to protect me from it. It wasn't your fault, Dhruv… It was never your fault, sweetheart…' She gently kissed him to cheer him up.

'I had no idea that you loved me so much,' she exclaimed. 'Dhruv, thank you. Thank you for loving me so much that when I close my eyes for the last time, I'll have no regrets whatsoever because I would have already got the love that one gets during a complete lifetime,' she said with a heartfelt smile.

Dhruv held her hands and cuddled her affectionately. He got emotional every time Emma mentioned about her impending end. Dhruv then opened a box and took out a special gem.

'What's this?' Emma asked with surprise.

'It's a special gem called Moonstone. I got it made for you,' he said.

'Wow…thanks! And what does it do?' she asked.

Dhruv paused for a second and then braving the torrent of emotions, he said, 'Emma, they say it gives peace.'

Emma smiled and said, 'I'll wear it, but you know what— my peace is right here with me.'

She kissed him and said, 'Dhruv, you're a very special person.'

Dhruv shook his head and didn't seem to agree.

'Look at me, Dhruv. You know why I've loved you all my life? It's because despite the ambition, passion and drive you've had in life to succeed and shine, you've always been even more truthful and warm. You make everyone around you feel special and the best part is that you are not even aware about your goodness! You sacrificed the New York film course, your career, your dreams for your Baba, and you've fought all your life paying off his debts just so his soul rests in peace. You've sacrificed a lot for me and you still think you could have done more. I always thought that someday I'll learn more about stones, gems, karma and yoga… Ugh…' she sighed regretfully.

'You know, Emma, reading about them has been a revelation to me. But my biggest learning is that one evolves the most not by reading religious and philosophical texts or performing rituals; the greatest spiritual evolution perhaps lies in the act of giving and serving others. Men live for themselves; sages live for others.'

'And what are you, Dhruv? Man or sage?' she instinctively asked.

Dhruv smiled and shrugged, as Emma continued, 'I'll tell you—you are a sage deep down, who is trying too hard to be a human in this world… Stop trying!'

'I am a human, I believe.'

'You've grown up, Dhruv,' she said.

'Did I have an option?' he asked. 'Back when I met you, I was this ambitious man who wanted to shine so bright that his Ma up there amongst the skies could see him. Ah…some dreams don't come true and that realization is perhaps a part of growing up,' he said.

Emma looked at him and said, 'You're going to shine one day, sweetheart.'

'Ah… I am done chasing dreams now,' he said.

'Dhruv, the best of things happen when you're not looking for them,' she said.

The Abode of Death

'I found you here in Banaras, thousands of miles away from my hometown, when all I was looking for was an interesting place for my documentary,' she smiled at how destiny conspired to make them meet. 'So, never say never! And, by the way, as far as your Ma and Baba up there are concerned, don't worry, I'll be meeting them very soon. I'll tell them how well their son has done and trust me, they will be very proud,' she sportingly smiled to cheer him up.

Dhruv broke down and said, 'Emma, I can't live without you... I just can't imagine...' His emotions got the better of him and he struggled to continue.

A visibly tired Emma said softly, 'Dhruv, don't cry... No, no, no... You're a brave man...'

Suddenly, her eyes seemed to be losing focus and she looked like she would faint. A worried Dhruv became alert and said, 'Easy, Emma... Relax.'

He immediately offered her some water but before she could drink it, she fell in his arms. A shaken Dhruv immediately lifted her as he observed that Emma's nose was bleeding. He shouted towards a buggy driver who helped them climb up, and they rushed towards the ashram. Emma was temporarily safe, but she was becoming frailer and more jaded with every passing hour. An intravenous drip gave her another lease of life, but the writing was on the wall. It was a matter of weeks, maybe days, as per the doctor's opinion.

Chapter 16

The Prophecy of Eternal Love

Dhruv sat by her side. He was gently pressing and massaging her feet. He would rub her hands, change her clothing and nurse her from time to time. Dhruv's pain was immeasurable and insurmountable, perhaps second only to Emma's. Watching your loved one disintegrate day by day was a soul-stirring experience for Dhruv.

The priest placed his hand on Dhruv's shoulder and asked him to come outside. Dhruv had stayed awake the whole night, sitting by her side. He accompanied the priest outside, and the latter offered him some food, which he gently refused. Dhruv sat down on a small ridge outside the ashram. He was tired and silent. The priest was getting worried about him as well.

'I think winter will set in early this time,' he said, trying hard to get Dhruv to talk instead of wallowing in a pool of depression and anxiety.

Dhruv's silence was, however, deep and deafening. The priest sensed that he was slipping into a state of shock. 'Dhruv... Dhruv...' he said.

'Yes?' he responded in a low voice.

'Kid, you're a survivor. This too shall pass,' the priest said emotionally, understanding fully well that his words would seem hollow in the context of Dhruv's sorrow.

Dhruv remained silent for a minute and then said in a small voice, 'It's all over, priest... All over...'

The priest didn't react. It pained him to see Dhruv breaking down so terribly.

The next day, Emma woke up to the sound of conches near the ghats. She felt better compared to the previous night. As she opened her eyes, she saw Dhruv right next to her.

'Dhruv, sweetheart, you look terrible,' she said.

Dhruv smiled and said, 'How does it matter... You're feeling better?'

'It matters, honey! It matters to me. Look, when I leave this world, I want to be in the arms of my tall, dark and handsome lover,' she winked. 'I want all the ladies to be envious of me,' she smiled.

A teary-eyed Dhruv smiled and caressed her hair, 'Anything for you! I'll up my game for you, sweetheart.'

'Good... I am actually getting better at having my way these days. I guess one gets spoilt during their last days,' she said, her voice gaining some strength.

Dhruv kissed her and said, 'By the way, today is a special day.'

'I could make that out from the sound of the conches early morning,' she said.

'Today is Janmashtami,' said Dhruv. 'One of our most revered Gods, Lord Krishna, was born on this day,' he said.

'Alright, I know a little about Lord Krishna,' she said.

'Really?' asked Dhruv.

'Oh yes. I am his devotee. He is the avatar of Vishnu,' she said with confidence, much to Dhruv's surprise.

'Wow!' exclaimed Dhruv.

Emma continued, 'And I love Lord Krishna as a mischievous kid, as a flute-playing romantic, as a warrior and, above all, as the messenger of the Bhagavad Gita. Ah Dhruv, I wish I could complete the Bhagavad Gita before leaving, but it seems unlikely now.'

Dhruv was always amazed at Emma's fascination for Indian culture and Hindu mysticism.

'Dhruv, I want to visit the temples. The Radha-Krishna temple, the Tulsi Manas temple, the glorious Kashi Vishwanath—all of them!' She requested this with a sense of urgency.

The two got ready and headed straight to the Hare Krishna temple, which was close to the ashram. The road leading to the temple was bustling with festivities and celebrations. The devotees were carrying beautiful and innovative forms of Lord Krishna on canvases.

'That's amazing!' exclaimed Emma. 'Hey, what's that?' she asked, looking at a small field down the road where hundreds had gathered. A decorated pot was hanging from a garlanded rope, as close to a dozen men huddled together with the chant '*Hare Krishna*! (Hail Krishna!)'

Dhruv smiled and said, 'This is another beauty of Janmashtami. You remember, Lord Krishna was a mischievous and innocent little kid?'

'Oh yes,' Emma remembered, waiting to hear more.

'Well, turns out, he wasn't that innocent as a kid,' Dhruv smiled. 'He would climb up walls and sneak into the neighbours' homes just so he could gorge on butter and curd.' Pointing towards another beautiful portrayal of the Lord during his childhood days, Dhruv said, 'Look at that!'

The Prophecy of Eternal Love

'Oh, he really was adorable!' Emma said, looking at a picture of the little Lord relishing his favourite butter.

'Yes, he was. So, every year on Janmashtami, we have young men competing to reach that earthen pot above.'

'Fascinating!' remarked Emma, as the rickshaw-puller manoeuvred towards the Hare Krishna temple. Inside the temple, the ambience was soothing and calm, contrary to the vibrancy of the roads outside. Emma closed her eyes in prayer as she tried to bow before the deity. She was struggling to do so, as Dhruv helped her. Her struggle continued as she wanted to ring the temple bell too. The determined girl that she was, she managed both with Dhruv's help. The two visited many temples and ghats that day and as they reached the Tulsi Ghat, Dhruv told Emma about Tulsidas, the author of 'Ramcharitmanas'. He also told her about Lord Rama, and his trials and tribulations.

'So, Lord Rama's idealism was his dharma?' confirmed Emma.

'That's right, Emma. He was righteous, just and an idealist on every front,' he said.

'Dhruv, what was my dharma in life?' she curiously asked.

Dhruv thought for a second and then said, 'Selfless love, Emma.'

Emma warmly held his hand. Her fingers were trembling due to weakness, but her touch exuded affection, as she asked, 'And what is yours?'

Dhruv despondently replied, 'I have nothing left, Emma. I always thought that my dharma was storytelling, but look what happened. I'm barely able to hold together my life. I don't even nurture any desires anymore. The only desire I wish could be fulfilled was of staying with you forever, but alas, destiny has its own script.'

Emma kissed him and said, 'You know not what destiny might have scripted for the next chapter of your life. You never know, Dhruv. Look at me, I never thought that my next chapter would bring me here, but I have no complaints from life. It has been a blessing all the way and I'm content 'cause in the end, it's all about smelling the roses.'

Dhruv was touched by Emma's goodness and her gratitude for life, despite all the injustice meted out to her by the cruel hands of destiny. Cuddling her warmly, he said, 'You're right, sweetheart. You're a blessed soul, who I was destined to meet.' Dhruv's emotions were finding their catharsis in his words, as he continued, 'All my heartbreaks and losses aside, I'll always thank the Almighty for bringing you into my life… Thank you, Emma.' Dhruv kissed Emma who was overwhelmed by his love. She experienced bliss as she reciprocated the affection.

They continued their spiritual pilgrimages for another few days. They visited the Kashi Vishwanath temple, one of the holiest temples dedicated to Lord Shiva. Emma discovered new facets and avatars of Hinduism. Dhruv even took her to a Durga temple, where they worshipped the Hindu Goddess.

Dhruv told her, 'Goddess Durga is invoked for her strength—Shakti. We believe that a woman has so much power that if she wants, she can defeat all the evils on her own. Goddess Durga is a manifestation of women's power in its most divine form.'

As the days passed by, Emma's will and determination began giving way to the onslaughts of her failing health. Dhruv would chant hymns and mantras for her peace and strength.

She would meditate for hours together just so she could be ready to depart from this colourful yet lacklustre world. And then there came a time when Emma just couldn't walk. She lay in her bed quietly. She had become pale. Her eyes had started losing their sheen. She had become painfully thin. Her digestive system had started giving way as she experienced a complete lack of appetite. Dhruv dreaded to think what might be going on in her mind.

He even asked the priest, 'Priest, what goes on inside the mind of a dying person?'

The priest told him, 'Nobody knows, Dhruv. It is beyond what writers, priests and poets can fathom. Our scriptures tell us that your next life is governed by your last thoughts.'

'What does that mean?' asked Dhruv.

'It means that if your karma was good, then whatever regrets or unfulfilled hopes you carry to your grave, manifest in the form of achievable goals in your next birth. You're born in the circumstances where you can fulfil those desires,' he said.

Dhruv was a bundle of contradictions. A part of him was too shattered to absorb any kind of spiritual wisdom, whereas another part of him was slowly and subconsciously understanding the nature of life, death and beyond.

For the next two days, Emma couldn't muster up the physical strength to step out of the ashram. She would meditate for long hours. The priest would chant hymns and narrate anecdotes, sitting beside her. Dhruv would rub her hands and feet. He would brush her hair, oil her feet and whisper sweet nothings in her ear all day.

The next day, Emma had an epiphany. That morning things seemed a bit different to her. Her attendant gave her a warm smile as Emma opened her eyes to the first rays of the sun. She could barely smile back. She, however, called for Dhruv.

Dhruv came inside and sat by her side. She gathered some strength and in a barely audible voice she said, 'Dhruv, I want you to take me to the Manikarnika Ghat.'

Dhruv wondered how Emma would make it till there.

However she was determined. 'Dhruv, just don't waste time.' The words seemed apocalyptic to Dhruv. His heart sank and his mouth dried up as he wondered what he should do. A moment later Dhruv agreed and called for a car. But Emma didn't want to go in a car as she felt it would hinder her from seeing, smelling and absorbing the essence of Banaras. However, Dhruv insisted and the two made their way to the burning ghat—Manikarnika Ghat.

Dhruv lifted her in his arms as the two descended the steps. The burning ghat was witness to hundreds of cremations and crying families every day. Dhruv had scarred memories of the place where he had lit his Baba's funeral pyre. As he sat down on one of the steps with Emma on his lap, he asked her, 'Emma, why did you bring me here?'

A visibly drained Emma smiled and said, 'Dhruv, tomorrow when I am gone, I want you to burn my body there.'

Dhruv's heart plummeted to unknown depths as he heard those chilling words.

'This place has given me so much, honey. It has given me a sense of karma and dharma, and you and the elixir of life. I want you to follow all the rituals when I am gone and once the blaze of my funeral pyre dies down, honey, collect my ashes and immerse them in the holy Ganges,' she said, struggling at every word and yet wearing a complacent smile. 'Will you do me this one last favour, Dhruv?' she asked.

Dhruv put up a strong front and holding back his tears, he kissed her ear and whispered, 'Yes, I will, honey.'

Emma's smile kept becoming more and more radiant as she said, 'Honey, the priest told me that the intuition of a dying person is very strong. I can feel that right now... I think my time is slipping fast now...very fast.'

She could barely speak, as Dhruv tried hard not to panic. Emma could barely open her eyes.

'Dhruv... One last stop,' she smiled, as a chill ran down Dhruv's spine. He nodded and sighed a couple of times but alas, the cruel hands of the ticking clock didn't even let him mourn. Time was running out for Emma, as she mustered whatever was left of her strength and said, 'Dhruv I want to see the Ganga Aarti one last time.'

Dhruv wiped his tears and kissing her forehead, he resolutely said, 'Yes, I'll take you there.'

After much struggle and pain, Dhruv managed to take Emma to the holy steps of the Dashashwamedha Ghat. As Dhruv gently carried her in his arms and descended the steps, Emma felt an exhilaration that was beyond words. She felt the comfort of a thousand cushions in his arms, as her light green eyes gazed upon a sight she had yearned for all her life. The sight of Dhruv against the expanse of the skies above, and holding her in his arms, filled her with unfathomable joy, as she peacefully smiled through the pain she felt every time Dhruv walked down a step.

Then, Dhruv gently lowered her on to a step, wrapped a blanket around her, and affectionately placed her head on his lap. Tears of joy were streaming down Emma's cheeks. Such was her happiness that her agony and pain paled in comparison.

Dhruv looked towards her with love and warmth, as he said, 'I love you.' The conches blew hard as he said those words. The temple bells too rang, as Dhruv kissed her. The chanting of hymns had started along the ghat. The lamps had been lit and the torches were set ablaze, as the Ganga Aarti commenced. Emma looked on with reverence and peace, as she absorbed the aura of mystique and devotion one last time. Cuddled in Dhruv's arms, she felt her life had come a full circle. Innumerable visuals and thoughts from her past kept flashing across her eyes.

She saw a beautiful, green-eyed, vibrant little girl jumping around and giggling across the meadows of Geneva, full of life, yearning for love. She then saw the little girl celebrating Christmas every year in her orphanage wondering who her parents were. She also saw her strange parents, who she forgave and to whom she gave away everything she had, without ever receiving any genuine affection in return. Her volatile marriage, which ended unceremoniously, her tryst with Banaras, and her journey of true love and peace, which culminated in Dhruv's arms... The visuals kept flashing as the chanting and music began to reach a crescendo.

Emma gradually started feeling light, as the rituals continued. She then whispered, 'Dhruv, I think it's about time now.'

As much as Dhruv tried not to cry, he gave in to his emotions briefly, before recovering his composure, and said, 'Emma, thank you for everything.'

Emma smiled and tried to touch his face. Dhruv was about to break down when she said the prophetic words, 'Dhruv, our love will never die. It is eternal.' These words seemed to be coming from a divine place. 'It will smile every time it sees goodness. It'll laugh every time it sees happiness. And this is the prophecy of eternal love,' she enunciated slowly. Her words had so much celestial magnificence that it seemed the cosmos itself stood still to hear them, and say, 'So be it.'

'Dhruv, coming to Banaras and meeting you was the best decision of my life,' she smiled, as her voice kept getting weaker. 'I have no regrets, no grudges, nothing but love and gratitude for the life I've had. So, Dhruv, remember me with a smile…remember me with happiness.'

'Smile' and 'happiness' were among her last words as Emma began closing her eyes. A melodious flute playing somewhere in the background, soothed her nerves. Some young boys and girls standing around them began humming the song, 'Kashi resides in our hearts.' Through her one last gesture, she asked Dhruv to sing along. He obliged and sang a few lines, barely able to control his tears.

'You're too good for this world, sweetheart,' he said. She smiled as he kissed her eyes. 'Your fragrance will spread all over. Your presence will reside in everyone's hearts.'

A smiling Emma bid goodbye to the world. Right there, in Dhruv's arms, she breathed her last.

The songs, the conches and the chants continued playing in all their glory, as Emma's soul left for perhaps some other world or maybe some other incarnation. Dhruv called her a couple of times. He even gently caressed her hair and her face, hoping against hope that she'll say something one more time, but Emma's journey in this world had reached its conclusion.

Dhruv looked around for some time. Perhaps reality hadn't sunk in. He didn't want to believe that it was all over, but Truth surely knows how to catch up and strike hard. A few moments later, it hit him like a thunderbolt as he started crying inconsolably. He hugged Emma's lifeless body tightly and kept sitting there on the steps for many hours. The passersby were moved by his unimaginable agony. Some even offered a gentle touch of condolence, but Dhruv seemed broken beyond repair. The priest soon got the news, as he came out looking for Dhruv. Dhruv's bloodshot eyes, crying in vain, shook the priest to the core. He was so devastated that the priest didn't even attempt to console him with any words. All he did was offer Dhruv a shoulder to cry on.

The priest bent and collected a handful of water from the holy Ganges. He came up to Dhruv and chanting a hymn, he sprinkled a few drops over Emma, praying for the peace of the departed soul. Dhruv looked up to the skies with pathos in his eyes and in a moment of catharsis, he cried out loud—louder than a bolt of thunder.

Chapter 17

Death of a Human

The next morning, Dhruv—true to his words to Emma—went to the Manikarnika Ghat to perform her final rites. The priest and other members of his ashram shouldered her body, wrapped in a satin cloth that Emma had chosen for her funeral just a day back. As her last journey began, the people started chanting, 'Oh Lord, it's the truth…the truth of death.'

As Dhruv undertook the long walk, he remembered how Emma had asked him to perform all the Vedic rituals. Her ever-smiling face, her hazel-green eyes, her vibrant voice and her golden heart… Dhruv's mind was flooded with her memories as he walked down the steps. The priest and others had started collecting the logs. A shell-shocked Dhruv was struggling to comprehend the rituals, but given that it was Emma's last wish, he performed each one of them with complete earnestness. He took a handful of water from the holy Ganges and sprinkled drops of it around the body, as the priest continued chanting the hymns. Garlands of flowers and rose petals soaked in the holy Ganges were placed on the body. Dhruv broke down multiple times during the course of these rituals, but the priest somehow steered him though the ceremony. Years back, the funeral of his father had left Dhruv listless and devastated, but this funeral had robbed him of his very purpose in life.

Shrouded in the satin cloth and placed on a bamboo stretcher, Dhruv looked at Emma's body, those eyes, those hands and that radiant face for one last time. The pyre was now ready—ready to be the final resting place of a body before it loses its manifestation. The chants continued and so did the tears from Dhruv's eyes as the moment of truth finally arrived. Emma's body had now been placed on the pyre. The logs of wood had one by one started concealing every trace of her physical existence. Her limbs were no longer visible, nor was her face—and finally it was all gone. Dhruv set the pyre ablaze with a torch. And then gradually, the wood started burning. The rising flames and the burning wood perfectly symbolized Dhruv's bruised mind and charred soul. It was all over for him. The fire kept burning, the people around stayed mum for a while and then as they say, the world moves on.

The rising flames meant different things to different people. For the log collectors, it was the validation of their sense of the right wood for the pyre; for the priest, it was a symbol of all rituals coming to fruition; for the beggars around, it was time to ask for alms; for many passersby, it was just another day in their lives. But for Dhruv, it symbolized the death not of an individual but of an identity. A part of Dhruv had died that day.

Dhruv sat near the place where Emma's body was burnt, silent and lost. Her ashes had been immersed in the Ganges with the hope that she would attain nirvana. The wind took with it some of the remaining ashes. Dhruv turned his head to

Death of a Human

follow their trajectory, but couldn't keep track.

He would sit there for hours and hours every single day; sometimes, even till the wee hours of the next day. He became so silent that one would think that he had lost his power of speech. But what was actually lost was his will to speak or express anything anymore.

The priest tried to comfort him but to no avail. He would sit next to him and try to speak with him, but Dhruv's deep silence was unbreakable. The priest, although an epitome of calm and rock-solid steadfastness, seemed shaken to the core. Days passed by, but Dhruv's stunned silence continued. The priest would offer him food, which he would politely refuse. He would sip some water intermittently but that wasn't going to help him survive.

'Dhruv... Dhruv... Listen, you've got to eat something, son.' He placed his arm around his shoulder. Dhruv stared ahead unblinkingly. He just seemed to be in a different zone.

So worried was the priest that during the routine praying sessions that he held with his disciples and protégées, he fumbled and missed the verses one day. He had never been so much out of sorts. He glanced towards the Manikarnika Ghat and saw Dhruv sitting there alone, despondent and motionless, and decided to go to him.

'Dhruv, listen... Emma always wanted you to remember her with a smile, right?'

Alas, it seemed as if Dhruv's will to live had also been immersed in the Ganges along with Emma's ashes that day. Visibly tensed and deeply introspective, the priest closed his eyes and meditatively contemplated about Dhruv. He remembered how, years back, he had prophesied glory and fame for the little child, who had survived despite his mother's death on an ill-fated day. Aghast at what had now become of that little boy who had grown up before his eyes, the priest sighed in despair, something very uncharacteristic of his generally stoic demeanour. He remembered how Dhruv had survived multiple setbacks and losses.

'The boy has to live on,' he thought out loud in a moment of prophetic epiphany, as he opened his eyes. It was a surreal moment for the priest who felt that he had a role to play in Dhruv's journey and his destiny was to make sure that the boy lives.

'You have to live on, Dhruv,' he repeated a couple of times with renewed zeal.

The priest brought Dhruv a plate of cooked vegetables and bread. He took a morsel of food and affectionately fed Dhruv with his hand. Dhruv was barely chewing. The priest, however, did not relent. He sat there for hours and kept cajoling Dhruv to eat. After much persuasion, Dhruv began moving his jaws, as tears started rolling down his cheeks.

The priest heaved a sigh of relief as a teary-eyed Dhruv slowly ate, while his gaze remained firmly set on the vast expanse of the Ganges. He didn't say a word, but such was the screaming intensity of his thoughts that every other sound, every other note, paled in comparison.

Chapter 18

Dhruv's Inner Thoughts

Today, I have lost everything. Every single thing that I ever held close to my heart has been wiped off by a reckless stroke of destiny. I sometimes wonder why...

All I ever wanted to do was tell great stories to the universe, make my parents proud and marry the love of my life. Then why did I suffer such callousness at the hands of fate?

Honestly, the explanations won't give me back my loved ones or losses, but they will, at least, provide some answers to the innumerable questions plaguing my mind. What could I have done to suffer such carnage and loss? I always knew what loss meant. My first step in the universe coincided with my mother's departure from this world. I never knew what a mother's touch feels like. The only thing closest to it that I had experienced was the cushion of my Baba's shoulders. The shoulders I could rest my head on and to whom I could ask countless questions, emanating from the innocent imaginations of a child. The shoulders I would stand on as a little kid to watch the glorious Ganga Aarti every year. But then, it wasn't long before I carried him on my shoulders to these very ghats.

Baba never ever hurt anyone. He was my father, my

mother and my best friend. Why was fate so cruel to him? Why did destiny take him away from me?

Tears began rolling down Dhruv's face, as he sat there motionless, impervious to everything around. He seemed to be lost in a parallel universe—a universe of his thoughts, his agonies and his countless, unanswered questions. The visuals at the Manikarnika Ghat kept changing and so did the hue, colour and ambience of the place, but what remained constant was a pensive, soul-searching Dhruv. This volcanic eruption of thoughts in his mind had engulfed him to a point where the outer world, the ghats, the temples, the grass, the wind—all seemed non-existent, as his cathartic dialogue with his soul continued.

> *Thousands of miles away from the Manikarnika, in the lush meadows of Switzerland, there lived a girl. Who could have thought that she would find her culmination along these same ghats where I am sitting? Our paths could've never crossed, but then strange are the ways of destiny... In Emma, I met a soul as pure as the holy Ganges. In Emma, I found true love—eternal and unfettered. Very rarely does one come across a soul as magnanimous, pure and forgiving as her's.*

Dhruv sat there for days, as the world around him moved on in a state of flux. He would question, introspect and seek answers about the vagaries of this world, and as he dug deeper into the innermost recesses of his mind, he seemed to be consumed by a vortex of realizations. Meanwhile, the sun would continue to rise every day, and the world would continue its pursuits, unchanged and unhindered. The rising sun's glory would gradually reach its highest point of the day and it would then taper off, and as the wheel of time continued, the sun would slowly dissolve into the Ganges, leaving behind a saffron trail, which would give way to darkness. However, amidst this darkness, there was an illumination of a ravaged soul, which had been meandering through abysmal depths and lows, seeking cosmic completeness.

Dhruv's soul cried and howled in agony, a chilling contrast to his palpable silence as he sat on the steps of the ghat. The priest was witness to this journey of Dhruv.

'He is going down, priest,' whispered one of his protégées.

The priest sighed and said, 'You know how pure gold is derived? The ore is pulverized, melted, moulded, pressurized and then left to cool for some time. And what we have then is pure gold.' The priest smiled and pointed towards Dhruv. There was belief in the priest's eyes—a belief that amidst the ruins of a bruised soul, there was a churning within, unfolding as per divine volitions. All he was waiting for was the culmination of this churning.

Dhruv's inner dialogue continued for days, graduating from mere ramblings to a divine quest. His epiphanies were more nuanced than ever:

> *Pain and pleasure—our entire cosmos is divided into these binary constructs. What if these binaries ceased to exist? What lies beyond the highs and lows, the ups and downs, the victories and defeats? Perhaps nothing but blank wilderness or maybe laced with this seeming wilderness there is a truth that eludes us—the truth of life, which*

cannot be pigeonholed into binaries, but is sought with complete submission and meditation.

The priest made sure that Dhruv was getting the required food and water to stay afloat. He would include Dhruv in the rituals that he, his co-priests and disciples performed. They would all practise thoughtlessness, a form of meditation.

Contrarily, Dhruv was entrenched in deep thought and he continued crawling along the unexplored realms of his mind. As it meandered through the alleys of darkness and grief, it also slowly set foot on the escalator of evolution, and gradually rose through the skyscraper of possibilities, regrets, losses and uncertainties, till it reached a zenith, beyond which was the expanse of the sky—clear and magnificent. His mind then galloped across the sky into infinity. It knew not where it came from, nor where it was going. All it experienced was the moment—the moment of existence; and the complete immersion of the mind and soul in the moment.

Dhruv would, at times, stay immersed in his thoughts for hours, long after the priest and others would come out of their customary meditative state. The priest was witness to what he called the turning of the inner eye towards light. Dhruv had slipped into complete silence—Vipassana, a form of meditation practised by sages to perfect control over their senses. However, Dhruv still struggled to govern his senses and hold back his emotions at times. He would occasionally cry out silently, thinking over the past. Sweating profusely, he would come out of his meditative trance in a bout of anxiety. So deep was his pain and so humongous were his losses, that it seemed impossible for him to conquer the agony and move beyond it. However, Dhruv seemed determined to rise above the binary construct of pain and pleasure, and march towards a realm of his mind that, till some time back, he didn't even know had existed. It was a realm of eternity; the realm of purpose.

The priest and his coterie held meditation sessions, undertook deep breathing exercises and performed chants, along with Dhruv. Vedic scriptures, the Upanishads and the Bhagavad Gita were recited and elaborate discussions called 'Shastrartha' were held. Dhruv would be a part of all the activities, but his stoic silence was unshakeable. Days and months passed by, but all that was ever heard from Dhruv was a serene echo of the Hindu religious chant, 'Om.'

With every passing day, the chants kept becoming deeper, calmer and more melodious. Soon, Dhruv started travelling along with the entourage of the priest from temple to temple, ghat to ghat on a spiritual journey. Dhruv's inner eye was gradually turning towards the light as he travelled through villages, towns and bylanes. Touring some poverty-stricken areas, he was also greeted with gut-wrenching sights of humanity suffering from extreme hunger and despair. It was at this point that Dhruv's spiritual quest acquired a divine purpose. Standing amidst the ruins of a thatched house destroyed by the downpour of the previous night, Dhruv looked around and saw little kids playing merrily, jumping around piles of wet straw. Their exuberance was in sharp contrast to their circumstances, and it was this contrast that summed up the delicious irony of life.

Dhruv also travelled throughout the length and breadth of Banaras, right up to the outskirts, till one day he reached the famous Sarnath temple. Legend has it that it was here that Lord Buddha gave his first sermon. There, Dhruv sat under a giant banyan tree. The sunrays, the breeze and the fragrance of the air, all felt different to him. He closed his eyes and started breathing deeply. The focus on his breathing was intensifying every passing second, as he started chanting 'Om' with a unique and unmatched serenity. It was a rare sight, as the priest marvelled at Dhruv's concentration. Drops of sweat began embellishing his forehead, which was criss-crossed with lines of wisdom.

And then, Dhruv felt an out-of-body experience. Deep in the state of meditative bliss, he felt as if a divine light had entered right into his consciousness from the cosmos. As it made its way, the light spread its radiance and magnificence through the contour of his being. The vibrations of this were felt by Dhruv, as he opened his eyes and saw a sight that would remain etched on his mind.

He saw the priest, his protégées and a handful of other devotees, praying and chanting hymns. He saw the temple bells at a distance. He also looked at the soil below, the terrain of the forest, the hovering clouds above—all of it appeared to coalesce into one visual, one entity and one reality.

And then, as if it was a divine pronouncement, he broke his silence after months and uttered the words,

'Jag mithya; Brahma satya.'

(The world is an illusion; the Creator is the only reality.)

The words echoed with resolute intensity as the priest and his protégées looked towards Dhruv, surprised that he had finally spoken.

One of the protégées asked Dhruv, 'How do we know, what is illusion and what is reality?'

Dhruv replied, 'Anything that erodes, withers and passes away with time is an illusion. Today, where we see roads and bridges, were forests once. The tall banyan tree was once a seed. Our forefathers are today a part of the soil or a part of the holy Ganges, indistinguishable and untraceable.'

'And what about reality?' asked another protégée, as the priest smiled and saw more devotees join the enriching discourse.

'Your karma,' replied Dhruv. 'It stays even after you're gone... Your dharma; it is within your soul, which is immortal.'

'What is dharma?' asked a devotee.

'Righteousness, sacrifice, service, selflessness, duty,' replied Dhruv, as the gathering kept swelling by the minute.

The questions kept coming in and Dhruv replied to them with a calm and insightful demeanour. The grief and sorrow that had engulfed him had slowly begun to loosen their grip and make way for an alluring and calm aura.

Dhruv closed his eyes for a second and chanted 'Om,' as hundreds joined him. Their chorus was as deep, melodious and pure as the holy Ganges. It was also the point of transcendence in the journey of Dhruv's life, as he got up and moved a few steps towards the entrance of the temple. A giant drum and a stick were kept outside. Dhruv had a spring in his stride and, at the same time, calmness was writ large upon his face, as he picked up the stick and hit the drum hard, followed by a thunderous Sanskrit chant,

'Sarve bhavantu sukinah, sarve santu niramaya.'

(May all be happy, may all be healthy, may no one suffer in any way.)

The crowd was abuzz as he drummed again and chanted,

'Ekam sat; vipraha bahudavanti.'

(Truth is one; sages and wise men celebrate it differently.)

Dhruv drummed for the third time and chanted another hymn,

'Seva parmo dharma.'

(Serving people in need is the greatest religion.)

The atmosphere was electric as hundreds of people had gathered at the Sarnath temple. Every time the stick struck the drum, a pearl of wisdom came out from Dhruv's soul. So thunderous was every beat that it seemed like a sign from the Gods, marking the birth of a legend. Amidst the charged atmosphere, Dhruv struck the drum hard one more time with elan and chanted a hymn that would go on to become the purpose of his life—

'Daridra Narayan seva.'

(Service to the poor and underprivileged is a service to God Almighty.)

The atmosphere was filled with a mystic energy as the priest, his protégées and the hundreds of people who had gathered were witnessing the reincarnation of Dhruv. Some called it Dhruv's rebirth, others called it his second coming, but history went on to judge this day as the moment in time when a legend was born—the legend of Guruji.

Right there at the Sarnath temple, under the fabled banyan tree, what started with a handful of people would go on to become a phenomenon that would resonate with millions across the globe.

Chapter 19

Birth of a Legend

Five years later. Jawaharlal Nehru Stadium, New Delhi.

The capital of the world's largest democracy and the power seat of a country with a population of more than a billion—New Delhi had its eyes on the famous Jawaharlal Nehru Stadium. It was packed to the rafters, as thousands waited for the commencement of a saga. It wasn't a rock show, nor was it a play or a ballad. They had gathered in record numbers to hear a man for whom a priest had once prophesied—'His words would make the Gods sit up and take notice.' A loud drumbeat signalled the beginning of the show. One beat after another galvanized the crowd as they stood up in anticipation. A couple of saints came forward and blew the conches. The atmosphere had a pulsating mysticism as the anticipation kept rising to a divine level. And as the sound of conches gradually faded out, the crowd broke into rapturous applause to welcome the man—the legend they called 'Guruji'.

With every single step, a multitude of thoughts flashed across Dhruv's mind. Dressed in a traditional silk kurta-pyjama, he gracefully walked down the aisle amidst chants and wishes. With a trimmed beard and neatly combed hair, he was unlike any god-man or conventional spiritual preacher.

'One day, I'll become so big that my Ma up there would be able to see me' echoed his past self as Guruji marched towards the centre stage and Dhruv matched him step by step in his walk down the memory lanes. Standing in the centre of the stage, he tried to let the moment sink in as he heard the voices from his past.

'Glory or fulfilment?' Dhruv asked Emma.

'It's all about smelling the roses, Dhruv,' Emma smiled.

The visions continued for a moment before Guruji spoke and the world listened.

'*Seva parmo dharma!*'

(Serving people in need is the greatest religion.)

In the last five years, Guruji, with the help of his millions of followers, had opened two thousand orphanages, ten hospitals and five hundred shelters for the homeless. His creed of selfless service to the needy reflected in his work and resonated with people across different faiths, races and strata of society.

Dhruv continued addressing the gathering. His flair for storytelling was intact and more potent than ever. Little did he know that his oratorical skill and mastery of words would enthral millions and get its due in this avatar.

'The universe has been divided over the concept of God. Is God a He or a She? Is God abstract? Is God a myth? ... Some are divided over other questions: Is there something called heaven and hell? Do we have just one life or do we have rebirths? ... And if this wasn't enough, we have different modes of worship. Some worship nature, some worship idols, some seek solace in the holy Ganges and some just prostrate before what they believe is their manifestation of God... But the fact is, *ekam sat; vipraha bahudavanti* (truth is one; sages and wise men celebrate it differently).'

Dhruv's address struck an emotive note when he asked, 'So what is truth? ... The one reality, the one common thread in every faith and every belief, is the creed of giving, the creed of service to the needy, the creed of kindness.'

The crowd clapped, as Dhruv's stirring address continued. Backstage, many saints and religious scholars listened to him carefully. Amidst them, stood an old, frail priest, who wore a calm smile, as he looked towards Dhruv. With tears of joy in his eyes and a certain charm still intact, the priest was watching one of his fabled prophecies come to fruition. He had known about Dhruv's destined greatness right from the day he was born. He was worried at one point, fearing that Dhruv would break down beyond repair, but Dhruv's indomitable spirit helped him to tide over the worst.

And then the priest witnessed the most amazing culmination of his prophecy.

Holding the mike in his hand, Dhruv looked around with a smile and said, 'You know, I come from Banaras, the holy land of the Ganges. My forefathers used to deal in stones, gems, pearls and other mystic elements. It was there that I had my first tryst with mysticism. Little did I know that it would assume the proportions that it has today.'

The crowd was riveted by Guruji's words, as he continued, 'There was this legend in our village that my forefathers were alchemists.'

The word 'alchemists' got the crowd murmuring. Dhruv closed his eyes for a second and remembered how this word had time and again come up in his life, right since his childhood.

He then said, 'They say an alchemist is someone who,

through his craft, can transform ordinary lead into precious gold.'

'Lead to gold...' the crowd whispered.

'I used to ask my Baba, "Is it possible? How can someone convert lead into gold? Is it a magic trick?" He would gently reply that the magic trick was none but penance and hard work. He would then tell me that I would know about it one day... The priest who held me in his hands the day I was born, had also prophesied that like my forefathers, I would be an alchemist. And I would wonder how I would convert lead to gold,' he said, sharing a good laugh with the audience. 'But, as life happened, I realized what the true meaning of an alchemist was... In life, we meet and come across many people, who leave their indelible stamp on us. Some of them change our lives forever. They transform the "ordinary us" into something precious and valuable to the universe. These agents of transformation are what we call the alchemists. So, today, close your eyes for a second and take a deep breath.'

The crowd followed the cue and closed their eyes, as Dhruv continued, 'And now, as you walk past the different alleys of your memory lane, think about that one person, that one magician who transformed you into a valuable and precious being.'

Many then asked Dhruv, 'Guruji, who is the alchemist in your life?' The crowd waited with bated breath for Guruji's reply.

Dhruv smiled and said, 'Years back, right on the banks of the holy Ganges, in my hometown of Banaras, I met a girl, who came to my life like a divine blessing. Her name was Emma. You know, before I met Emma, I was this ambitious person who believed in glory more than anything else. I wanted to be the shining star in the skies above. Little did I know that "fulfilment" was far more important than "glory". Guruji sighed for a second and then went on, 'Emma often said that it's all about smelling the roses.'

A mesmerized crowd was at the edge of their seats as the combination of a storyteller Dhruv and a mystical Guruji captivated their attention.

'She breathed her last, right in my arms, and I couldn't stop her from going. In that moment of helplessness, I realized the lesson of submission—submission to the will of destiny and God. But before she left, she told me something that transformed me forever. She said that our love was forever, and it would remain long after she was gone. It is eternal. It'll smile every time an act of kindness is performed. It'll breathe every time an aggrieved soul gets relief. It'll sing every time a dream or the desire of a poor child is fulfilled. And it'll cry every time a plea for help goes unheard.'

Charged with emotion, the crowd listened with rapt attention, as Guruji continued, 'Just hours before dying, she made a prophecy—the prophecy of eternal love. So pure and honest was that prophecy that it came true, and today, every time I open an orphanage or a hospital or a night shelter, I feel the heartbeat of our love. Every time a poor child gets to pursue their dreams of studying in a school, I see Emma smiling from above. The prophecy of eternal love has come true,' Guruji reiterated, as the crowd erupted in thunderous applause.

'People ask me who I am—am I a god-man, a religious preacher? And I tell them that I am an alchemist. I try to be an agent of change in whatever capacity I can be. If I can help a little child get an education, I'll be an alchemist for him. If

I can look after the abandoned, then I am an alchemist for them. And trust me, people, it is a feeling like no other. So, go home today with a resolve to be an alchemist for someone. Be an agent of change in someone's life because the truth is that service to humanity is the greatest religion—*seva parmo dharma*.'

Conches were blown and the crowd cheered for Guruji.

Dhruv's company, The Alchemists, had become a charitable foundation. It was only symbolic that what was started as an attempt to revive his father's ailing business, had branched on to become the biggest charity of the country. The Alchemists raised money from across the globe for charitable programmes like girls' education, orphanages, cleaning polluted rivers and helping poor farmers. Dhruv's sessions drew large crowds all across the globe. His mantra ('Be an alchemist'), comforting replies and counselling sessions had become hugely popular. Politicians, heads of states, businessmen, all lined up to meet Guruji for comforting words of encouragement.

Guruji addressed gatherings all across the globe and as destiny would have it, he was eventually invited to speak at the New York Film Academy. Standing on the dais, he addressed a group of young students.

'How much does this admission, this seat in the premier film institute of the world, mean to each of you?'

'It means a lot!' was the unanimous answer.

Guruji nodded with a smile, and said, 'You know, years back, there was a young kid—a gifted storyteller, they say— who got a full scholarship to the New York Film Academy. It meant everything to him. All his dreams, his desires, were right there in that envelope, which he remembers till today. But alas, he came from a very humble background. He didn't want to leave his ailing father alone either, and with a heavy heart, he kissed the offer goodbye.'

The gathering curiously asked, 'And then?'

Guruji replied, 'And then he failed… He failed so badly that he was left devastated and heartbroken. But you know, there is this thing about failure—failure is never final. Life took him through loss, pain and failure.'

'Where is he today?' asked a young girl from the crowd.

'Today, he is standing right in front of you,' he said with a disarming smile, much to everybody's awe and surprise. 'And the one takeaway for him was that nothing teaches you more than failure. Failure is the best teacher that you can have as a student. Failure is also the muse of a storyteller. The pain, anguish and loss takes our mind to unexplored territories, where some of the finest jewels are mined and brought forward to the world.' He spoke from the heart and captured the imagination of one and all.

Dhruv's juggernaut continued to thunder through the globe. He was posed different questions concerning life and dharma. One such question at an august gathering in Mumbai was, 'Why is there so much suffering in the universe?'

Guruji replied, 'That's the one question that gave birth to countless sages and priests. If not for the suffering and pain, religious preachers and spiritual gurus would've not even existed. Suffering is the first step towards an awakening. But why does suffering exist in the first place? There are broadly two kinds of suffering in the world. The first one has its roots in desire and attachment. If you desire a particular lifestyle, wealth or stature in life, and you end up falling short, you get disappointed, dejected and begin to suffer as a consequence. If you are too attached to your possessions and you forget that everything is temporary in this world, then you are bound to suffer the day you lose them. The good part is that this kind of suffering can actually be controlled by disciplining your senses. It's difficult, but doable. Meditation and yoga were born to address this kind of suffering. Then there are remedies as outlined by Lord Krishna in the Bhagavad Gita—"Equanimity in pain and pleasure is true yoga". The day you're not too overjoyed with success or pleasure, and neither are you too dejected with pain or sorrow is the day you're on the right path to yoga.'

The crowd absorbed every word from Guruji, as he continued, 'The second type of suffering is beyond man's control. It has its roots in death, disease and old age. A young man, righteous and honest to his family, meets with a tragic accident and leaves his young wife and small children behind. That's a tragedy beyond comprehension. A young girl at the start of her life is diagnosed with a terminal disease. These are the tragedies that no one can explain. Lots of theories in different faiths have been postulated to address this kind of suffering and tragedy. However, I refuse to be convinced by them.'

Guruji's replies sent shockwaves across the audience. Here was a religious preacher, a god-man, who openly said that religion did not convince him on this subject. But then, it was this sort of practicality that made Guruji so different from other religious preachers. The moderator asked Guruji rather hesitantly, 'Guruji, are you saying that religion doesn't have this answer?'

Guruji promptly replied, 'You're right, I totally believe

that no religious text or theory justifies the suffering of an innocent child or a young father. This is where religion has its limitations and we must accept it rather than offering grandiose theories and justifications.'

'Then what does one do, Guruji?' asked the moderator.

'Count your blessings, every single day,' replies Guruji. 'And remember, if you are blessed and privileged in any way, it becomes your duty to share that blessing with the not-so-privileged. Be an alchemist, an agent of change, for the hundreds and thousands who, without any fault of theirs, are suffering in abject poverty, disease and exploitation. As for a desire-led suffering, I just have to say—rise above!'

Chapter 20

Salvation Truly Lies Within

*A*fter every session, Guruji would be thronged by people asking for personal meetings and counselling sessions. He would try his best to oblige as many as possible. One day, as he retired for the evening and went back to his room, one of his attendants came up to him and said, 'Guruji, there is one person who is desperate to seek your counsel.'

'Tell him that today's session is over and he is most welcome to come to our ashram tomorrow. Give him an appointment,' he said.

'Pardon me, Guruji, but the man looks to be in deep trouble. He was crying for help and he seemed totally broken,' reiterated the attendant. Guruji then asked him to send the man to him.

Guruji, meanwhile, rested on a sofa and browsed through the contributions by various people for his foundation. A few minutes later, the attendant knocked on the door, and with Guruji's permission, he brought in a man who seemed dispirited, devoid of any zest for life. He was in his sixties, with a dishevelled beard and droopy eyes. He seemed a bit familiar to Dhruv, as he took small, nervous steps towards Guruji. There was anxiety and lack of confidence written large upon his face as he bowed in front of Guruji.

Then, as he raised his head, Guruji looked him in the eye, and a moment later, he asked him, 'So, what brings you here?'

The man started speaking rather anxiously. 'Guruji, I... I...,' He was fumbling as Guruji placed a hand on his shoulder and calmed his nerves a bit. The man was on the verge of breaking down. However, he somehow collected himself and said, 'Guruji, I wasn't always this miserable.' He spoke with trembling lips. 'I was "the man" once upon a time, you see. I had the whole world lining up just to catch a glimpse of me, just to see me for a coffee or a meeting.' The man was beginning to open his heart, as Guruji carefully listened.

'I was at the epicentre of all the glamour and glitz. Film premieres, launch parties, wine and women—I had it all. They called me the maverick film-maker,' he painfully smiled, reminiscing about his lost glory. 'And then it all went away, sank without a trace. Today nobody knows me. My films bombed one after the other. I never really had a family, to be honest, but the one woman for whom I had done everything, Laura, too, left me in search of greener pastures... That bitch!' He sobbed and cursed.

Regaining his composure, he said, 'But you know, Guruji, despite all the losses, the one thing that eats me up from inside and makes me feel hollow is guilt about a crime I committed years ago.'

The man seemed at a loss for words, as he trembled with anxiety and his guilt-ridden voice wavered. 'Guruji, years ago, I robbed a young boy of his dreams and livelihood.' With tears in his eyes, he said, 'You know, Guruji, my most accomplished work, *The Most Successful Failure*, for which the world hailed me as a genius, is actually not my work, nor is it my ex-girlfriend's. It was written and narrated to me by this young boy from Banaras. I can never forget those eyes, straight and piercing like an arrow to the heart. They haunt me every night when I try to sleep. I can never forget those eyes...' he said with anguish.

As he lowered his head and cried in desperation, Guruji went a step ahead and put his hand on his shoulder. The man then slowly lifted his head and looked straight into Guruji's eyes. He rubbed his eyes to clear what he thought was his blurry vision. But what he saw in those eyes wasn't a mistake, but the truth—the bitter truth from his past. Surrounded by lines of wisdom and a skin that was radiant though a little shrivelled after many a winter, Guruji's eyes had the same resolute intensity that a twenty-one-year-old Dhruv had when he was robbed of his dreams by a callous maverick.

That 'maverick'—Zubin Mistry—had today been reduced to an anonymous entity, helplessly seeking solace. As Zubin looked into those eyes, tears started pouring down his cheeks, and he trembled with fear and anxiety. He folded his shaking hands together and begged for forgiveness. A tear rolled down Guruji's cheek, as his past flashed before his eyes, but then the worldly wisdom that the same tumultuous past had taught him got the better of it and he said, 'Salvation lies within.'

This sentence was the essence of the story that he had written, and it also summed up the wheel of karma in this case. Zubin cried desperately and fell on Guruji's feet.

'Guruji, I am your sinner. Punish me, kill me for what I've done,' he shouted helplessly.

Guruji helped him to get on his feet and politely said, 'Zubin, that's not the solution. Will punishing you bring back the formative years of my life, which I lost out on? Will it bring back a promising career that was aborted right in the womb? Will it give me back my dreams, my life? The answer is no.'

'But Guruji, I want to end my life. I cannot live with this guilt anymore,' he cried out.

Guruji smiled and said, 'Zubin, this is the wheel of karma. Ending your life will not be the solution, because karma chases you, life after life, birth after birth. It shall rest only after its purpose is achieved.'

'So, what should I do, Guruji? Should I tell the world that my best work was actually written by Dhruv? I'm ready to do it today,' he said.

Guruji smiled at him and said, 'Dhruv died a long time back. His essence, his soul, remains alive in me. You telling the world that it was Dhruv's work won't do any good to anyone in the universe today. You've lost so much credibility and relevance that your words may be dismissed as gibberish or unbalanced. They would fall on deaf ears and, most importantly, this issue is buried so deep in the obscure past that it is virtually worthless to reveal it now.'

'Guruji, please tell me what should I do then?' Zubin helplessly asked.

'Repent... Repent not by crying and feeling miserable, but by promising me today that you will not allow another Dhruv to die at the altar of some callous film-maker. Promise me that you'll help some Dhruv in some corner of this country to realize his dreams. Be an agent of change for him—be an alchemist and that will be your true repentance,' he said.

A grief-stricken Zubin cried till long after Guruji had gone; he cried all through that night. However, the next day, was a new dawn for him as well. He started serving in Guruji's ashram where he would train and mentor homeless children in various arts and crafts.

Guruji would often visit the old priest, the one constant in his life since the day he was born. The priest was probably the only person who had seen from close quarters the death of Dhruv and the birth of Guruji. The priest's old eyes would always light up with pride every time he saw Guruji, and the two would often have a heart-to-heart discussion.

'So, how did it feel to see Zubin after so many years?' asked the priest, sipping a cup of warm tea.

Guruji thought for a second and then replied, 'Nothing... I just didn't feel much at all. You know, priest, that man destroyed my life and livelihood. And he was right there in front of me, vulnerable and helpless, but I just didn't feel any anger against him. I had felt bad and sad about what happened to me years ago, but surprisingly I don't have any grudge against the man, now.'

The priest looked at him gently and smiled. He had become pretty weak over the years. However, his sense of humour was still intact. 'Is this the same person who had last time around slapped Zubin across his face telling him where salvation lies?' he laughed.

Guruji shared his laughter and said, 'Who is that person you're talking about? I don't know him.'

The priest laughed out loud and said, 'Well, I know him and I've known him always. He is pure gold—twenty-four carat.'

Guruji smiled warmly at the compliment and just when he was about to bow in respect before the priest, the old man stopped him. After a little struggle, the priest got up, limped a couple of steps towards Guruji and made a priceless gesture—smiling at Guruji and marvelling at his journey and stature, the priest bowed before him. Guruji rushed to stop him, but the priest insisted. 'My Dhruv has come a long way,' he cried with tears of joy, as the two hugged and savoured the moment.

That night the priest slept well. Nice and warm, he dozed off so peacefully that he never got up. Guruji performed his final rites along with the other priests and his students. The wheel of destiny continued revolving, as Guruji immersed the priest's ashes in the holy Ganges.

Guruji's popularity by now had assumed epic proportions; ironically, so had his nonchalance towards fame and popularity. He no longer cherished worldly success as his conscience kept evolving spiritually.

'Guruji, when does the cycle of life and death stop?' asked an attendant in one of the sessions.

'The cycle of life and death ends with salvation. Salvation lies within. It happens when both pain and pleasure cease to affect you,' Guruji said.

'Does there come a day when pain and pleasure truly stop mattering, Guruji?' asked a devotee.

Guruji thought for a second and with an affirmative smile, he said, 'Yes, there does come a time when the binaries of winning-loosing, pain-pleasure, cease to matter. You evolve so much that everyone and everything seems to be one universal truth and that's when you know that your worldly purpose has been achieved.'

That day, Guruji's words emanated from various thoughts doing the rounds of his mind. They were peacefully coalescing into something big.

Chapter 21

Be an Alchemist

Guruji's foundation had today become an institution in itself. Guruji wanted to appoint trustees to ensure that The Alchemists would continue its good work long after he was gone. It was a huge event in Banaras, along the ghats. Politicians, representatives from human rights organizations and the United Nations, and corporate heavyweights, all had lined up for the event at the famous Dashashwamedha Ghat. Guruji's devotees and followers had come from over a hundred countries. A makeshift stage, tastefully decorated with local artefacts, was set up.

As Guruji took to the stage, the crowd broke into rapturous applause. It was like a sea of supporters, each of a different hue in an already colourful evening. Many followers from various far-flung countries had stories to share about how Guruji had transformed their lives.

Guruji smiled and wondered how, years ago, destiny had ensured that even in the most intense legal battle over his family business, Dhruv managed to retain the title of his firm—The Alchemists. He was robbed of everything by his wicked uncle, except for the name. Today, it was only divine justice that The Alchemists had become a name and a creed that inspired millions across the globe.

As for Dhruv's uncle, Vidur, he had passed away a couple

of years ago. His last wish was forgiveness from Dhruv but alas, he breathed his last, minutes before Guruji arrived.

As the glittering event unfolded and a banner with 'The Alchemists' written on it was hoisted fifty feet above the ground, the crowd got on its feet and chanted '*Har har Mahadev!* (Hail Lord Shiva!)' Legend has it that Mother Ganga's abode was in Lord Shiva's hair, and it was the Lord who introduced the holy Ganges to the Land of Dharma—India.

Amidst a charged atmosphere replete with divine chants and the sound of conches, the crowd welcomed Guruji to the dais. His aura seemed paradoxical to the people. His warmth made him relatable, but at the same time, his magnanimous persona made him seem like a distant dream to millions. He virtually held the audience in the palm of his hand.

Guruji thanked the thousands who had arrived from different countries on what was a historic day for his foundation. He then said, 'I've always been fascinated by the word "eternal". Eternal love lives on long after the lovers have separated. Eternal goodness is undiminished. Any creed or emotion that is eternal is independent of time, age, era and dimension. Today, ladies and gentlemen, I wish to declare before you all, that the noble creed of The Alchemists shall also be eternal.'

The crowd applauded thunderously. Guruji then began the process of anointing the trustees of The Alchemists foundation. The media was abuzz with inquisitiveness and so were large sections of the gathering. As the trustees were announced, the applause continued and they gracefully accepted the honour from Guruji.

The glittering extravaganza continued as mediapersons

jostled to get the adequate coverage. As Guruji stood there, calm and peaceful, he felt a certain nip in the air. He had a divine epiphany of sorts as he looked around. It was something inexplicable and incomprehensible. Perhaps it was an intuition about something significant waiting to happen. It was then that Guruji heard a couple of mediapersons talking loudly amongst themselves. There was a certain vibrancy and pulsating excitement in their behaviour. The rest of the audience was getting inquisitive to know what the enthusiasm was all about.

And then, one of the mediapersons stood on his toes and called out loudly, 'Guruji! Guruji!'

Guruji looked at him and so did the thousands gathered there.

The mediaperson then said, 'Guruji, I just received a confirmation from the news desk. Your name has been recommended for the Nobel Peace Prize.'

Those words echoed resoundingly in Guruji's ears, as he stood there and wondered. It was as if his entire life had come full circle. After years of yearning for success and glory, Dhruv's moment of glory came at a time when he had moved on and graduated to become Guruji, an apostle of renunciation. Guruji smiled at the irony of life, but the remnants of Dhruv inside him shed a tear of joy, as he looked towards a star-studded sky. It was as if the stars had lined up for this moment to salute destiny's favourite child.

A roar of excitement and applause followed, as a chant of 'Long live Guruji!' filled the ghat.

Guruji's smile didn't waver and he absorbed the magnificence of the moment. However, he soon realized that even a moment this pure and glorious couldn't stir him.

Perhaps he was rising above pain and pleasure, on the path to spiritual enlightenment.

Within minutes, the news began flashing across various channels and on social media. The clamour for Guruji's bite went through the roof, as everyone from prime ministers to presidents sent out congratulatory messages. The international media too took notice and wanted to get a bite from him.

In sharp contrast from this media glitz and glamour, Guruji was seen visiting one of his schools the next day. It was one of the hundred schools run by The Alchemists, situated right behind Guruji's ashram.

Apparently, he had learned that a little boy had fainted during one of the lectures. He entered the staff room to check on the boy, who was surrounded by a fellow student, a teacher and an attendant. Guruji looked at him and then signalled everyone to leave the room. Guruji then shut the door and very softly said, 'Listen, kid, I know you're acting, so please get up.'

The child, in his innocence, tried even harder to lie still. Guruji smiled at his naiveté, and in a friendly yet stern way, he said, 'It's not working, mate. So, get up.'

The little boy rubbed his eyes and got up the next minute.

'I'm sorry Guruji,' he said avoiding eye contact. 'But Guruji, how did you come to know?' he wondered aloud.

Guruji sat next to the little one, and said, 'Kid, you need to act better. I could see the corners of your mouth breaking into a smile.'

The little boy sighed in vain, 'Oh Guruji, I try so hard, but my friend, he starts laughing, and seeing him, I'm also not able to hold my laughter.'

'Oh! So this has been going on for quite some time?' Guruji asked.

'Sorry, Guruji,' the boy apologized and lowered his gaze. He was about to cry, when Guruji lovingly patted his shoulder and asked, 'So, tell me the truth. Why do you do this?'

'I'm sorry, Guruji, I try my best not to do this but...,' he said hesitantly.

'But...' said Guruji.

'But Guruji, the lecture is so boring! So, so boring that I can't tell you,' the child reasoned. 'Guruji, I tried everything. From trying to keep my eyes wide open, to pulling my ears, but nothing works in this lecture,' the boy continued, as Guruji listened intently.

'And then Guruji, my friend and I came up with this plan—'

An amazed Guruji guessed his plan and completed his sentence.

'Plan to faint in turns and avoid the lecture,' said Guruji.

'Correct,' smiled the boy.

'And Guruji, sorry, but this plan really works,' he laughed.

'I know that,' Guruji laughed out loud.

'But Guruji, how do you know?' he asked excitedly.

Guruji smiled and reminiscing about his childhood days, said, 'Always cover your face when you are acting, it helps. And listen, from next time, no more fainting.'

The boy laughed and obediently nodded in agreement.

'What's your name, kid?' asked Guruji.

'My name is Gopal.'

'Gopal, what do you want to become when you grow up?' asked Guruji.

'I want to be rich, Guruji. My parents are very poor,' he said.

Guruji lovingly patted his cheek and said, 'What does

your father do? What's his name?'

'My father's name is Sudama. He works in a factory.'

'Sudama...' repeated Guruji with surprise.

'Yes, Guruji, and we come from the village Bhadarpur,' he said.

Guruji smiled. A floodgate of memories dating back to his childhood days had opened up. He and Sudama were best friends separated by fate. He remembered that day when Sudama left the school. Guruji's eyes welled up as little Gopal softly enquired, 'Guruji, are you crying? ... I am sorry, Guruji. From next time, I'll not faint in class,' the boy apologized with folded hands.

Guruji smiled and hugged the little one. He then said, 'Gopal, will you take me to your home?'

A bewildered Gopal asked, 'Really, Guruji, will you come to our house?'

Guruji nodded and said, 'I want to go now.'

Gopal's eyes lit up with excitement. He jumped with joy at the prospect of Guruji visiting his house. He held Guruji's finger and walked with him towards his home. Guruji's aides and associates were surprised to see him as he went through the bylanes to the shanties of Bhadarpur.

Little Gopal had a spring in his steps as his friends and neighbours saw him with Guruji. It was a poor village with unpaved roads and crumbling infrastructure. People came out in droves to see Guruji. Gopal's joy knew no bounds as he blissfully smiled at the attention he was getting. The news had spread far in the village, and it had by now reached the door of Sudama.

Sudama was surprised and wondered why a Nobel Prize nominee would come to visit him. Poverty-stricken, he was embarrassed by his rather humble abode.

As Guruji knocked on the door, both Sudama and his wife came out to welcome him. A visibly poor and humbly dressed Sudama opened the door rather nervously. It was too overwhelming for him to welcome a man of Guruji's stature to his modest shelter. A sense of inferiority and a tinge of embarrassment was written large upon his face. As he came face to face with Guruji, he folded his hands in reverence.

For Guruji, it was a moment he had never expected would happen. He held Sudama's hands and warmly hugged him to everyone's surprise. The onlookers were surprised by Guruji's gesture. Sudama was overwhelmed and startled beyond words.

Sudama's wife, Meneka, said, 'Guruji, I hope Gopal isn't troubling anyone at school.'

Guruji replied, 'Well, I do have a complaint against him.'

A worried Meneka asked, 'Guruji, what has he done? We will ensure that it doesn't happen again.'

Guruji smiled and said, 'Well, what he has done is something I'll share only with your husband in private.'

Sudama then ushered Guruji inside and with folded hands, he said, 'Guruji, please make yourself comfortable. We will do whatever we can to discipline him, but please don't throw him out of school. I know what it feels like to not complete school. I don't want him to be like me, ever.'

Sudama then reluctantly asked Guruji to have a seat on an old dilapidated sofa. 'Guruji, I apologize, but this sofa is all we have,' he said.

Guruji waved a hand to silence him. 'A home is not built by beautiful furniture; it is built with love and warmth. And a home that is witness to little Gopal's mischief can never be poor; it is priceless.'

Be an Alchemist

As Guruji sat there, Sudama's wife Meneka went to the kitchen to get something for Guruji. She was struggling to decide what to offer. Her old utensils also embarrassed her.

Sudama was about to sit down near Guruji's feet when Guruji told him to sit next to him. A visibly surprised Sudama once again folded his hands and said, 'Guruji, I'm sorry for Gopal's mistakes. I don't want him to be like me.'

Guruji smiled and said, 'But he is just like you.'

'Pardon me, Guruji'? said Sudama.

Guruji said, 'He is just as bad an actor as his father was when he was young.'

Sudama wore a puzzled look as he wondered about what Guruji had just said. 'Guruji…'

'Sudama… At least now teach your son to not smile when he pretends to faint,' Guruji said, laughing heartily.

A bell rang in Sudama's mind and tears of nostalgic joy began rolling down his face.

'Dhruv…' he whispered.

Guruji nodded and said, 'Class V, Section C, St. Mary's Junior School.'

Sudama hugged his old friend and broke down. Overwhelmed with joy, he said, 'I always knew that my Dhruv was going to be a big man one day.'

Guruji smiled and said, 'Big or small, in the end it doesn't even matter.'

An elated Sudama then asked, 'I don't know what to call you—Guruji or Dhruv?'

Guruji replied, 'Today, after years, I have met someone who knew Dhruv before Guruji took over. You're probably the only one who remembers Dhruv, so call me that.'

Sudama hugged him again and said, 'I can only refer to

you as Guruji now. Calling a saint like you by your name would be highly uncivil.'

Guruji smiled and shook his head in disagreement, but Sudama insisted on calling him Guruji. His wife Meneka too got emotional on seeing the reunion of the friends. She had always heard stories of a certain Dhruv, who used to be her husband's only friend in school. Today, she witnessed Dhruv in an avatar revered by millions across the globe.

Sudama and Meneka went to their kitchen to get something for Guruji, but all their utensils were worn out. However, Meneka quickly made her favourite curd rice with the limited resources that she had. Standing in the kitchen, she told Sudama, 'That's all we have in our house.'

A bit embarrassed, Sudama said, 'I feel bad serving this to him. How many times have I told you to buy some decent utensils in case any guest comes!'

'And how many times have I asked you for money to buy them!' she cried in despair.

Guruji overheard those words. He was pained to see his friend in abject poverty. As he sat down, a thought came to his mind. He opened his purse and took out a valuable stone he had had from the time he was a little boy. It was the same red stone given to him by his father before he had died. Ram had said that the stone would protect him through thick and thin. The stone had been a part of Dhruv's tumultuous journey and was also witness to Guruji's ascension. Today, this rare stone was worth lakhs in the market. Guruji had cherished this prized possession all these years.

Sudama and his wife reluctantly served the rice to Guruji. However, Guruji tried his best to allay his friend's uneasiness. He sat down with them and relished the rice served by

Meneka, saying, 'People think that the right ingredients of a delicious meal are the correct spices, salt and pepper. But they are wrong. The right ingredients are love, hospitality and the warmth with which it is prepared and served.'

That day, Guruji ate to his heart's content. Happy and satisfied with the meal, he called Gopal and said, 'Remember, your father is a great man. All his life, he has toiled hard against many odds only to ensure that you have a great future. So, study hard and love your parents. They are your biggest well-wishers.'

Little Gopal listened intently and nodded in agreement. He then touched Guruji's feet. Guruji blessed him with happiness and prosperity. On that note, he took leave of his friend Sudama and said, 'Clear the dishes carefully.'

Sudama couldn't quite fathom what Guruji meant at that time. However, when Sudama went back to the table where Guruji had eaten, he found a small bundle wrapped with paper, under Guruji's plate. It was a bit heavy. On unwrapping it, he saw a red stone inside it. Along with the stone, there was a note left by Guruji. It read:

Dear Sudama,

Thank you for the wonderful meal. I feel blessed to have met you and your family. Years ago, I could not do anything for my friend when he was forced to leave school. That sight has haunted me for years. Today, life has given me an opportunity and I don't want to let go of this moment. This stone was given to me by my father, and it kept me safe all these years. I often wondered why I never sold it, but I guess destiny had its own plans. Kindly accept this gift from your friend and I'm sure proceeds from its sale will help you in giving a great future to little Gopal and his dreams. Always live with your head held high, Sudama.

With love,
Dhruv

It was after years that Guruji had signed off as Dhruv. He made this exception for his best friend from childhood. Sudama's eyes welled up as he sat down for a moment to absorb what he had just read. He called over his wife. The two looked at the stone and marvelled at the magnanimity of the gesture.

'What a life-changing meal it was!' Sudama wondered aloud, kissing the stone.

Guruji's gesture had just changed Sudama's fortunes forever. It was pure alchemy—the creed propagated by Guruji.

Chapter 22

It's All about Smelling the Roses

Meanwhile, Guruji's nomination for the Nobel Peace Prize had received huge support across the entire political spectrum. The buzz and campaign to celebrate his award were unprecedented. Ironically, the stronger the buzz, the more nonchalant was Guruji's attitude. He was content and at peace with himself.

And then came the official news of the award: 'Guruji would be awarded the Nobel Peace Prize on 25th January'. It was a moment of widespread celebration across the country. The award would be presented in Oslo, as per the tradition. Guruji's disciples celebrated with pomp and show. The media clamoured for a bite from Guruji. However, they were told that he had undertaken the fast of Vipassana, and would remain silent for days together. The news of the prize had reached his ears, but he remained entrenched in meditative bliss. Days passed by but Guruji's silence remained unbroken.

The date of the award ceremony was approaching, as the frenzy in the media had reached great heights. However, the instruction from the ashram was to keep the paparazzi away.

A couple of days before the ceremony, Guruji finally ended his meditation and called over one of his disciples, giving him a letter sealed in an envelope. The disciple looked at Guruji and with tears in his eyes, he prostrated before him and sought his blessings.

The day had now arrived. The first rays of the sun were yet to break through the clouds. It was going to be a special morning for a multitude of reasons. Guruji's entourage had reached Norway. The cameras and paparazzi were itching to catch a glimpse of him. However, they couldn't find him anywhere. They thought that perhaps he would come separately, but the reality was far from that.

Before the break of dawn in the holy land of Banaras, Guruji walked out of his ashram. In the wee hours, he was in his janmabhoomi (birthplace) and karmabhoomi (workplace), Banaras, thousands of miles away from the glitz of the award ceremony. It was three o'clock in the morning as a calm and serene Guruji walked down the Manikarnika Ghat.

Over the years, this ghat had been witness to some of Dhruv's most painful moments. Guruji stood there for a minute and closed his eyes. He remembered those endless questions that he innocently posed to his Baba. He also remembered telling his Baba, 'I want to shine so bright that my Ma from up there can see me.'

A magnificent smile adorned Guruji's face, as he continued walking around the burning ghat. In that stretch, countless memories floated around in his mind. He could almost touch each of them and watch them play on the theatre of his mind.

'It's all about smelling the roses, Dhruv…' Emma's words rang in Dhruv's mind.

A few steps later, he remembered how he had performed the last rites of Emma and his father. A further few steps and he vividly remembered the birth of Guruji, which took place at Sarnath.

Guruji was watching his entire life replay in front of his eyes as his walk continued. He just kept walking… It wasn't an ordinary walk by any stretch of the imagination. It seemed as if the entire cosmos was witnessing the divine catharsis of destiny's favourite child. Dhruv kept walking through the ridges and bylanes and towards the forest.

Thousands of miles away, in sharp contrast to the spiritual silence of Banaras, an inquisitive paparazzi had by now run out of patience, trying to catch a glimpse of Guruji. As the day commenced and the historic hour arrived in the Oslo City Hall, Guruji was still conspicuous by his absence.

However, miles away, Guruji had never felt more present. Every pore, every organ of his body seemed to feel the celestial energy.

As the Nobel Prize ceremony commenced, everybody was curious to know where Guruji was. Little did they know that he had transcended to another spiritual dimension.

As Guruji's name was finally about to be announced, the crowd and the media became quite impatient, longing to catch a glimpse of him. However, he was nowhere to be seen.

The moment finally came, and Guruji was declared the official recipient of the Nobel Peace Prize. Amidst thunderous applause and to everyone's surprise, Guruji's disciple stood up from amongst the crowd.

'Where is Guruji?' everyone was asking.

His disciple climbed onstage and stood behind the podium. He took out a letter and placed it in front of himself. He then greeted everyone.

'Thanks to the eminent jury for bestowing this honour

upon Guruji. But ironically today, Guruji is not here for this ceremony and I also cannot accept this award on his behalf. What I can do, however, is read out this letter written by him and addressed to all of you. If I have your permission, may I?' he asked.

The committee allowed him.

I thank the Nobel Prize Committee, my friends and my supporters from across the globe. Today, I am not there, but hopefully my words will reach you. As big an honour as the Nobel Prize is, I very humbly decline this award.

The crowd and the committee members were puzzled at what they were hearing. 'Guruji turns down the Nobel Prize,' read the live headlines. His disciple, however, continued reading.

Ladies and gentlemen, my life today has come a full circle. Today, I have no regrets, no grudges and no complaints. I started as a little boy who lost his mother as he came out of her womb. I always wanted to shine like a star. Glory was my motto, but little did I know that life had other plans. I've seen debt and death from close quarters. I know what it feels like to be robbed of your dreams and I definitely know what heartbreak means after my loved ones died right in my arms.

However, destiny kept me alive despite every loss and every setback. It kept me alive because, through me, it wanted to give everyone a lesson for the ages. And that is—it's all about smelling the roses. It's all about gratitude. Be grateful for what you're blessed with, because there is so much more to lose.

Through me, it wants to tell you to keep going, no

matter what. You never know when the stars might line up to acknowledge your hard work when you least expect it.

And above all, through me, it wants to tell you that 'alchemy' is real. Be an alchemist, be an agent of change for a human, and help them transform into gold.

Every single day, when I saw our foundation, The Alchemists, transform lives and bring smiles to many faces, I knew that I was the richest person in the world. It was a reward far greater than even the coveted Nobel Prize. Destiny also chose me for a very special purpose. The trials and tribulations of life got me thinking deeply about life and human existence. And I realized with every passing day that I was graduating in my pursuit to rise above pain and pleasure to reach a point of eternal peace and bliss. I knew that if there came a day when I touch this chord of meditative bliss, I shall have outlived my worldly purpose.

Today, that day has come. I shall not see you all again. But you'll see me smile every time you do an act of kindness, you'll hear my chant every time you help an underprivileged, and you'll have my blessing every time you undertake the pursuit towards meditative bliss.

God Bless you all!

Lots of love,
Guruji

There was pin drop silence amongst the audience. The mediapersons, the viewers across the globe, everyone was stunned after hearing Guruji's words. There was hardly a dry eye in the audience. It was a surreal experience.

After a minute of silence, a round of applause erupted amidst a section of the audience. Others joined in, and in a matter of seconds, there was rapturous applause all across the hall. This resonated across the globe as Guruji's supporters both applauded the great soul and grieved his departure.

His devotees searched for him everywhere. They looked in many ashrams and on the ghats, but Guruji was nowhere to be found. A boatman claimed to have last seen him at a temple near Manikarnika Ghat.

It's been ten years since that day and still nobody knows where Guruji is. Some claim to have seen him in the mountains, others claim that they have seen him in the jungles. The only truth is that Guruji's presence is felt every time an act of compassion and kindness is performed. His ideals continue to inspire The Alchemists and his legacy of eternal love and magnanimity continues to be revered by millions.

The legend of Guruji lives on…

Acknowledgements

So, this moment is finally here. As you read this, I want you to know that I'm filled with gratitude towards God and the universe that I could accomplish what I had set out to, around four years back on a cold winter night. I remember that day as if it was yesterday. I was fresh out of the success of my first novel, *Jack & Master*. Life was unfolding at a feverish pace. My career as a public speaker was picking up and I was addressing large gatherings of students and professionals.

I could have written a college rom-com or churned out a campus story as my next, but somehow I wasn't getting a strong voice from within. However, life had its own surprises lined up in the coming months. My Uncle's betrayal towards my family, which would shake one's belief in goodness, and a failed relationship were rude shocks awaiting me in the course of my life. The crests and troughs of life set me on a path of soul-searching. It was a tough time, but as they say—the darkest nights produce the brightest stars. And it was on such a dark winter night, when I was staring at the star-studded sky that the idea of Dhruv dawned on me. That night, I decided that I will rise above all obstacles and odds to tell this story of grit and determination to the world.

In this journey, there have been a few pillars of support who helped me sail through the turbulence:

Top of the list is my Mom. She is the biggest blessing of my life. Thank you mom for giving me the most amazing upbringing. Every single word that I write for a book and every single speech that I make on stage, is dedicated to Goddess Saraswati above and my mom here on earth.

I have to thank my Dad, who has supported me one hundred percent in all my pursuits. The simplicity with which he has conducted himself in business and life is an example for me and many others.

My sister, Divya is one of the most courageous and brave persons that I know of. She is a total gem who shines ever so brightly and her positive energy keeps everyone around her in good spirits. No matter how low I'm feeling, when she lovingly calls me 'Sitara'—star—I feel alright.

I am grateful to my friends and well-wishers who've been with me through thick and thin.

I also wish to thank the team at Rupa Publications for their support.

Lastly and most importantly, I would like to thank you—the reader. You are the one I wanted to share this story with, and today, as you hold this book in your hand, my dream has come true. Today when I'm past the tough phase of my life, I can tell you that I'm stronger and wiser than ever before, and the one thing that I have realized is that your dreams are precious and they're always worth fighting for.